Journey of Two Hearts!

D1439879

WITHDRAWN

And what a mother says – a son for a mother and a man for life partner is everything in her life. When he is happy, it fulfils all her dreams, but when he's sad even for a moment, it takes her life away. It's the greatest and the luckiest feeling in the world to be a life partner or a mother.

Journey of Two Hearts!

will be cherished forever

Anuj Tiwari

Srishti
PUBLISHERS & DISTRIBUTORS

Srishti Publishers & Distributors
N-16, C. R. Park
New Delhi 110 019
editorial@srishtipublishers.com

First published by
Srishti Publishers & Distributors in 2012

Fifth impression 2015 (revised)
10 9 8 7 6 5

Printed and bound in India

"Getting the best person in life might make a good love story, but falling in love with the stupid one, and making that person best makes a hit love story."

To Pakhi's family

and my parents, who gave me the best quality of DNA

because I enjoyed when life lived with me,

and survived when everything seemed lost.

And those people who left me with no reasons.

Loving someone is not tough, but the real courage is
to be with that person…forever.

Acknowledgement

Who says, luck is written by God. I just checked; it's still editable. People always used to laugh in my school days because I was not like those modern boys who used to play with costliest toys and went to high class schools. I can remember when I was 10, I prepared a speech and in the middle of the speech, I forgot those tough English words which I had mugged up a night before. Everyone started laughing and I felt like crying. But it was more painful when my own classmates laughed at me. I could only remember one thing that my mother had said – never give up. Patience has its limits and I couldn't sustain; I cried at the next moment. I never discussed that awful day with anyone as I thought my mother would shout and feel awkward. That day I learnt one thing – when the sky cries, birds start chattering; then how can you expect that people won't laugh if you cry. Life is yours and it's up to you how you take and how you make it.

I always wanted to do something different from the crowd, but how and what was a big question. When I was a kid, I used to say to my mom, 'I want to do something different in my life'. And every time my mom slapped me and put me back to my studies. I started my life with a very normal school. When I grew, my family decided to make me a good engineer. It happens in our society – if your neighbour is a doctor or an engineer, you have to be one of them. Sadly, I had both. So I was sure, either I'd be an engineer or a doctor. Everybody was running in the race of engineering from the day one till the day they got the offer letter from some multinational company. Life seemed gold-coated iron and I never wanted to be a part of that crowd as neither I forgot 'to do something different' nor my mother's slap on my face.

My dad used to tell me when I was a kid, one day we all have to sleep forever, so let us work till the day we breathe. That time I considered dad's philosophy, but now those words give me courage to stand once again whenever I fall in life.

Picking up the pen and writing this true tale has had some reasons. Before I become more sentimental and go ahead, my heartfelt and genuine thanks to all the names I take here, to whom I'll forever be grateful for taking me ahead in the journey of writing this tale of my life.

Mayank, Ankit and Ankur, thank you for being with me from the day I used to ring your doorbell to go for tuition classes.

Anushka for helping without reasons.

Love you, mom, dad and di for watching over me always and for listening to me – for the support that went beyond this book. Moreover, thanks to all who unflinchingly gave me their hands to hold.

In addition, my friends who did not trust me and kicked out from their life in my bad time, I want to say thanks to them. Somewhere they put courage and passion in me to go ahead in life.

Thanks to the whole team at Srishti Publishers for publishing me and listening to me whenever I flagged queries.

And the most special thanks to the adorable readers who loved me so much and supported me. Love you all, muah.

A lot of love to the cities I spent a few years of my life in:

Bareilly: For bringing me up with affection and helping me learn how to be happy with small things in life.

Lucknow: For always treating me like its own son and giving so much love.

Kanpur: Where I spent a year of my life and learnt about friendship.

Guna: The place that made me an engineer of machines and a narrator of my own life, and for those treasured memories of college days.

Delhi: This place gave me memories to remember for the rest of my life.

Bengaluru: The city of lovely romantic weather and wonderful people, especially the walk in the evening.

Mumbai: Last, but definitely not the least, Mumbai is known as the city people come to for fulfilling their dreams, and I know it to be true.

Prologue

Hi Anuj,

Please read this mail with patience. Anuj, I know we have had a lot of fights in the last few days. I wanted to share a lot of things with you, but we couldn't talk about it. Either we were too busy romancing or too busy fighting.

For a girl, her love is her world, and she tries everything to make her love happy. A girl never gets into a relationship to get involved physically, but still she comes close just to make her love believe that her soul is now dedicated to him.

I know I'm the reason of all the fights but it's also true that I love you a lot more than anyone in my life.

I just want to love you forever, but whenever I changed myself for our love then something went wrong and then I stopped doing anything for our relation. Anuj, I love you a lot and I want you to be happy. Please remove from your mind that I want to leave you.

Why would I leave you?

We love each other so much and there is no reason to leave.

A guy who takes care of everything in my life, why would I leave him?

A girl wants a caring, understanding, loving guy in her life and you complete me and make my dreams come true every morning with your love. It's a dream for a girl to be with you and I am the lucky one.

Anuj, you are the one who wakes me up early in the morning, who sings for me before I go to sleep, makes me laugh whenever I feel sad and makes me cry with his lovely surprises.

You pamper me like a small kid as my dad used to do. I can see him in you, that's why sometimes, I talked to you very rudely. Truly I'm nothing without you Anuj. I can't even think my life without you. I want your eyes to see the success, your words to get self-motivated, your lips to make our future smile, and your shoulder to sleep.

Hope after reading this, we'll have a tight hug.

I'm waiting for your hug.

Your Loving,
Pakhi

Ring the Bell

I stretched my body, tiredness on my face; I looked at her. She smiled at me serenely, and with the grandiose of a tortoise her hands gracefully inched towards 1.00 am, consequently letting out a loud shrill as one metal surface crashed against another continuously. My clock had often symbolized the times that life in hostel and life at home could never be at tandem, yet one existed because of the other. With parents around things were porous, even cordial. In a residential engineering college though, the culture brimming was entirely different. Projects, study time (whether exams or no exams!), birthday nights with bumps, crowded rooms during exams, fight for a *samosa*, bets on girls, while nobody had guts to say *Hi*. It effectively churns out a weird breed of Asian species called 'Engineers'. It was obvious to say- *Engineers wake up when the rest of the world sleeps.*

We had always abided our motto. We were in full vigour at the dawn of 15th February 2009. It was the most romantic season, when the days were affable and the nights were cold and frosty. It fuelled the spirit of wanting to roll in the blanket or hang out with friends at the campfire after the sunset. I was accompanying my engineering books that night to finish Prof. Joshi's assignment. Prof. Joshi was one of them who believed in my intelligence and gave full contribution to change our life from 'Yo' to 'Oh'

There are few more things apart from diabetes which are hereditary like- if your father is an intelligent creature; there are high

1

chances to get the same quality of DNA in you and surety to be abused in friend circle at those instances whenever you score well or more. Luckily or unluckily I got the same, and the reason, Prof. Joshi had high expectations from me in upcoming examinations.

As all assignments were aimed to be completed overnight, as the deadline would near along with the rising sun, this one was no exception. At the end of three hours and thirty pages of work, my new roommate Uday and I were still struggling to finish it. Moreover, like so many proceedings, all the hard work that was pumping into the assignment was done with unwanted and semi-attentive mind. It got worse when I heard there were low uninterrupted knocks on my door. This kind of knock usually sounded like unwelcomed trouble. It was usual from last few days as being one year senior, Uday was completely involved in managing Fest Utsav 2009 and his physique gave him sensational charm to bring out fire in new-comer females from different part of the country.

Uday and I were sharing the same hostel room this year. We became good friends because we were from the same city Bareilly, and on my first birthday when everyone came to celebrate my birthday and basically to beat me, he and his localities friends saved me as that fun turned into a big fight. Though later on for next four years my birthday was the coolest birthday in the college but they were always hot and never left any chance to celebrate. 'Who is this?' looking at the door with tired eyes, I asked.

'Hey it's me,' a counter voice thundered from outside and clinking on the handle of the door, I could hear.

'But who's this?' I enquired again with no movements.

'Hey you scum, it's me, Maddy,' irritations in his voice clearly cut through the door.

'Hey, wait, coming,' I replied trying to release myself from blanket and books. Maddy was the frat star, he was always having a good time.

He had his own friends, so he wasn't needy and was cool. He used to live in squalor with way more guys than there should be. He used to stay out drinking until the booze is gone and especially he had tendency to get into fights. Door opened, Maddy staring back at me, alone, and as usual looked like a terrorist with Chinese moustache and Small Goatee.

'What happened?' I enquired. A red mark on his neck made me curious to know what interesting happened again for a girl. He screamed and walked in.

He glanced around, and in the same high pitch, 'Oh assignment! Keep it up lads.'

'What did happen to your neck?' I asked casually.

Tilting his head hardly to my side, Maddy replied in his too loud and clear voice, 'Nothing, just a small fight. But now it's all fine.' I laughed and patted on his back, 'So who left the battle this time.'

'Leave it, *behen ke takke...* Mofos,' he picked water bottle from the table which was about to lose its last leg the way Uday jumped on it last night.

Uday and I laughed. 'What is mofos?' asked Uday, we hadn't heard anything new in last few days except porn movies of which Uday had latest collection from Sunny Leone to Sasha Grey.

'Motherfuckers, you bitch,' Maddy laughed, and settled down listening motionlessly to the slow scratching of pen on paper, papers ruffling aimlessly, thoughts wandering helplessly. He started singing a song by Akon- 'Lonely, I'm Mr. Lonely...' rotating phone in between his fingers. I was not wondered that how he was enjoying his life without a whiff of tension as I scratched off and jotted down random shambles. Suddenly, sitting motionlessly, Maddy asked to sing a song.

'Song for you, never and by the way, I have to finish this off, that Banerjee will give me minus marks if I don't submit by tomorrow. I'll only sing for my dream girl,' I cracked a joke. DREAMS FOR A

DREAM GIRL…LOVE…ALL TIME TAMASHA. He jumped at the other side of the bed and said, 'And that dream-girl won't come ever in your life. So don't show me your attitude,' he commented and gave a punch on my shoulder and continued, 'Where is the guitar?'

Time had changed, *true-friends* was just a term in the inspirational books but at the other side I wasn't so unlucky so I got these insane, mad and crazy friends and life started becoming a *college-life*. I started singing and the room got a silence more than class.

```
She was in rain
But she wasn't mine
When I look at her
Everything goes fine
I wanna love you baby...Come to me...
I wanna love you baby...Come to me.
She was in rain
But she wasn't mine
When I look at her
Everything goes fine
But my heart wanna say one line,
May be you don't love me
May be you don't look at me
But I promise you baby,
You will be mine...Only mine....Only mine.
Just wanna say baby, o baby, o baby.....just
wanna say baby.
Come to me...
```

With those frets, he was shaking his body till the time my fingers stopped. 'Happy,' I looked at him.

'Hey Anuj once more please?' Maddy said.

'Now go to hell, I have to complete my assignment okay.'

'Hey just kidding my baby,' Maddy kicked on my ass and sat next to Uday to the other side of the bed. I didn't know what were they talking about but after few minutes, Maddy came to my bed, 'Have you completed your assignment?' and continued, 'Dude. Why are you so serious about the assignments? Just Copy and Paste it.'

'Maddy! I'm not going to do any Copy-Paste,' I retorted. He shrugged, took my cell phone, and overlooked bulk of missed calls and messages that flashed, ignoring them; he forwarded two-three messages to his cell phone. There was no Whats App so messages had their own importance.

After an uneasy silence he spoke to me directly, 'Hey, do you want to talk to a girl? But please don't let my name out.'

I admitted, I was single and was ready to mingle, but I was not the person who can call and chat up just about any girl. I ignored him. He tried again, looking at me very curiously this time.

'Hey just ask her name.'

'This is so unlike Maddy, people sleep at this time,' I finished the last line of the second last question of assignment.

'Look it's going to be okay. We're not sleeping, are we?' he said seemingly looking at number and punching it on my cell phone. The tableside clock said 1:20 am. 'It's over a quarter past one! In the midnight, if you're not sleeping it doesn't mean the whole world is not sleeping,' I replied pointedly.

'Hey just ask her, and ask what did happen with Paras,' he said, pressing phone on my left ear.

'Who's that girl and who's this Paras? Moreover, why are you so frenzied to know about her life?' I raged as a ring shot in my eardrums and my heart began to race. Uday sniggered. It seemed he knew about it before.

'Her name is Pakhi Maheshwari,' he said.

'Just ask her what I said. You can do this for me. Hold it now bummer, it's ringing,' he said urgently letting the phone go. A cold chill ran through the calves of my legs. I had never done this before. I pressed 'speaker' button and the ring reverberated across the now dreadfully silent room. He snatched the phone back, and pressed 'speaker off' button again and gave me. 'I don't think, anybody will pick the call at this time dude,' I ventured again.

'Wait for couple of more rings,' Maddy persisted, biting the nails out of his finger. Next moment she picked the call. She could be suffering from cold, but I chose to believe that she was sleeping and was rudely awoken at midnight. She said firmly, 'Hello?'

I waited for few seconds, 'Hello. Is this Pakhi?'

'Who is this?' a girl with sleepy voice asked.

'Are you Pakhi?' More giggles. She disconnected the call. I stared at screen, call summary: 00:00:10. Maddy snatched the phone, and fell himself off the bed, this time rolling with laughter, 'Such a sod.'

'Then why don't you try it?' I yelled at him this time. I watched helplessly as he bent low and went into a silent fit of laughter. I turned to find Maddy again dialling her number, and passing phone over to me.

'Wait. Why can't you do this?' I asked looking at Maddy.

'Because she has already heard my voice before,' he replied.

I added, 'C'mon, man. Don't you feel insult?' I looked at him flustered. I tried again and ended with the same result. Unable to contain myself, I hurled a proper series of abuses at Maddy finishing with, 'Now are you happy?'

'Oh you are such a bozo,' he said throwing my phone on the bed. I frowned. 'If I'm the bozo then why are you using my phone to carry out this ridiculous conversation?' I yelled.

'I have to sleep guys. Good night,' I said. Maddy walked out, seeming as agitated as he was, when he walked in.

When they were LOVING, when they were KISSING, when they were having... yes correct... SEX with each other, we were completing assignment on 14th February, the Valentine's night and this was our day and then something happened...

Horn Ok Please

If you are married, and have babies, you have to wake up early morning to change nappies because these days these responsibilities are shifted to males because our women are leading. If you are married and still using condoms, your morning is always wet. If you are single and still living with dreams with your hands, never wake up so early.

It was Sunday, just after the Valentine's Day, 15th February 2009; I woke up at 7:45am. I woke up to the dots of sunshine dancing across my room from the window through the lace of my curtains. The texture of the sheet against my skin felt good, warm, and cozy. I could hear movement downstairs of Uday and others going for breakfast. As I looked outside, the vast foggy sky met the rolling green hills. I attempted to peer out of the glass window but the cold from outside had created a fog making this difficult. I exhaled and watched my breath turn the cold morning air white. Somewhere I was still stuck in the conversation I had just few hours back with that girl.

'Should I say sorry and clarify my mistake? Or I can just ignore it,' I gave a thought to it. It's always good to say sorry if you have done mistake or sometimes even when you haven't done any. That shows your attitude towards life and people. I had become enough mature and decided to call her or her voice was good to hear again. As it was done from my cell-phone, so I had her number. Being comfortable, relaxed, I just hit redial button and disconnected. This got repeated multiple times as I was still not sure to take a valid decision in between womanhood Vs hormones-hood. As per the womanhood, it's not good to call an unknown girl and hormones-hood allowed me to know her response. As always, I couldn't do anything against the bumping of my hormones and I dialled. At the other end, I heard an alto.

'This must be her voice,' I guessed it next moment.

'Hello, who's this?' she questioned. In a slow voice, like a lazy wimp guy, I replied, 'Hello.' She questioned one more time. Before her voice went harsh, I responded, 'Ma'am someone gave me your number, so I called you in the night.'

'Who has given you my number and why? And who are you?' She enquired and shot these questions in seconds but politely. Girls are polite when they don't know the thing, once they get the idea, it changes their voice. After a syncing pause I replied, 'I'm sorry, but I can't tell his name.' Very confidently, she replied, 'Okay fine, but I don't like talking to strangers.' Phone was still on my ears, but line was disconnected. Again, I dialled her number, felt comfortable than the last time when I dialled her number, I was courageous now. She picked the call after passing more rings. I tried to make her comfortable by saying sorry once again. Relations are not maintained on sorry and apologies but sometimes they work in a magical way. 'Tell me who gave you my phone number,' she enquired again.

'Do you really think I should tell his name, I can't tell,' I requested this time.

'Fine then disconnect the line and don't call me again, ok?' aggressively she replied.

'Ok, you can disconnect the call,' I said and waited for her to disconnect the call but it didn't happen.

'You've called me to say sorry but you're not telling me who gave you my number. Being a girl what should I understand of this, you tell me,' she said.

Delhi girls are not only fair with faces but also with fair minds. I didn't think much and said whatever happened last night.

'Your friend Maddy gave me your number but you promise me, you won't call him now. I trust you,' I requested, took a big risk against the friendship but risks are important to fix. 'Ok, I promise you, I'll not tell,' She replied very freely.

'That duffer, but how does he know my number? How do you know him?' She was logical and nice at her each word so I explained her everything that happened though I was prepared and knew that something would happen for sure. Whatever she told me about him changed my perception towards him. To get results according to actions, I wasn't happy and shocked. He always used to tease her as she was pretty and intelligent. It made me frenzied to know more.

I asked, 'Were you friends?'

'He was my classmate for two years, we were only competitors,' she answered.

I mentioned 'friend' but I wanted to know more about both of them, as I knew, the most 'loving person' becomes 'enemy' in life, so it was just a check point.

'Someone is calling, I have to go, talk to you later,' she replied, no affection in her voice, disconnected the call.

Seems good, when a girl says, talk to you later that means she is giving you time after sometime.

'Just talked few minutes and searching affection in her voice, stupid fellow,' my mind said.

I laughed. I didn't want to lose the opportunity to talk. I said, 'I want to talk to you something important.'

'What, tell me?' asked she.

'Now you can go, but may I call at this number after sometime when you are free?' This time my tongue didn't slip to say these words.

'Ok, I'll inform you when I'll be free.'

'Ok, bye'. Phone line disconnected, I rose off in my cozy bed. I covered myself in rust brown and pink colored blanket. Once again, she smiled at me serenely, and with the grandiose of a tortoise her hands gracefully inched towards 8.30am. I looked outside, from the back door of the room. One hand was on my waist and other was holding the phone, I was standing in the balcony of my room. I looked at those small mountains surrounded with dense fog in the morning breeze. Chattering of birds, I was only able to see the edge of the sun in the fog. I sat comfortably on the chair in balcony, connecting both the hands to the back of my head pointing out, and looking at the blue sky. The sun was growing slowly as the time stopped for few moments, spreading its shining by showing mercy with warmth. I started a good morning.

After having *Samosa* in Sunday breakfast, I pulled out the phone that lay beeping in the right pocket of my denim. Automatically reaching for her number on the 'Recent Calls' list, I saved her number. I twirled my phone between thumb and the middle finger, and then shoved it into my pocket. Happiness slowly filled in as I thought I had found a friend; she seemed loving and caring enough. It was too early but my mind made a map. I waited till the evening but didn't get any message from her as she said she would inform once free. That night, I laid curled up in my cozy bed, the entire conversation automatically reeled an umpteenth number of times in my head. I wondered, as I changed sides and let out a determined sigh to focus on the sleep evading me.

'Could I have been more humorous, just to impress her further? Was the call perfect or not? Was my way of talking good? Would Pakhi be thinking about the conversation too?' I questioned myself. I predictably, didn't want to discuss this pleasant moment with others. Alone in my room, I was smiling at nobody in particular, and there was different sort of feeling within me. 'Why are you so excited and frenzied to talk to her again? Then I realized I was such a foolish guy but true with my thoughts. I looked at the mirror, which always listened me, 'Relax dude. There is always a tomorrow.'

Delhiites

Next morning, I woke up bit early, I tried to look at the clock, and rose my neck from blanket, and next moment clock rang. I threw it under the pillow but that was not enough to knit the dreams again. This was the time to clean out the old nest. I kept my eyes closed and stayed in my bed. I put my hand under the pillow and looked at cell phone with half opened eyes. I didn't check any messages, which were flashing on the screen and just messaged her, 'Hi.'

I was staring at my phone and waiting for her reply but I had gut feeling that she wouldn't reply. When God made females, he put lots of love, care, beauty and small amount of attitude and this is reason from Mahabharat (even before that) we fight for woman. *Don't make them feel that you are going crazy for them; just give some time and they'll come to you.* I was still uncertain on whom to turn to –heart or brain. Both of them were pointing in opposite directions, one wanting to satisfy my ego while other wishing to hear her voice.

Answer came from my heart and I neglected the proposal of my stupid mind. I went ahead and dialed her number, even though it was little early for that but what was late or early, didn't matter. She received the call. 'Hello,' said she.

'What's up?' I asked.

'Nothing.' Soon it dawned that I had nothing up my sleeve to draw about her against her, but she seemed to have a repository of 'unsolicited' information stored; information she could have obtained by those who have deceived me. These girls exchange information as fast as (some geek network stuff). 'Are you in Delhi?' I prompted. She took some time, 'Yes, I'm in Delhi and doing B.Sc. in Life Sciences from Hansraj College, Delhi University.' She stressed on last few words. A seemingly confident girl, answers just kept pouring in, never dry never gushing, she associated her college Hansraj with SRK.

'Ok any more information?' She asked.

'Is she choking me?' Delhi girls are enough smarter than guys. So it could be the part of joke, I thought. She wanted to know as I took to silence to fit in all the surge of facts. She was still giggling for some godforsaken reason. Do all girls giggle so much? I made a mental note to raise this in the next guy-discuss-girls meeting; must be discreet, of course.

'No that's fine for now,' I finished smiling. Before she could chock me more, I introduced myself, 'By the way, let me introduce myself Anuj Tiwari from Bareilly.'

She seemed smiling, 'My name is Pakhi Maheshwari from Debai, Aligarh, in Delhi from last three years.' What are the prerequisites, when you are talking to girls that from where she is, where she lives and what are her hobbies. Though I knew it all that she was from Debai <a small town in Aligarh, Uttar Pradesh> and she was in Delhi at her Uncle's place just after completing her schooling. However, there were lots more things to know, just like how does she look? Slim or fat? I thought for a while. I twirled fork in the Maggie and grinned looking somewhere in the room.

I asked, 'So must be enjoying your college days.'

She exclaimed, 'Yessssss!' Multiple S showed the truth of Delhi colleges and gorgeous Delhi girls. Moreover, giggled that gorgeous giggle again. It silently echoed on the walls across and reverberated back at the receiver end again. 'And at your end, just study right?' she amused. I wished that I could have something interesting to say and the things I had weren't supposed to discuss with her, that was purely 'Boys stuff.'

. 'Noooo, it's not like that.' I also put multiple Os in the answer forcing her to believe that we also enjoy in the college.

'We enjoy, but only in the hostel because there is nothing outside the college. We're not as lucky as you are,' I purred.

With her honeyed voice, she laughed, 'Yes, good place for you guys to study.'

Videos don't work every time to satisfy, sometimes you need real beauty that college rarely had. There was one is to eight ratio to fight for a girl, not less than any other competitive exam. This much effort if I could put before coming to engineering college I could hopefully get of the IITs and after that I could get any model with perfect figure. Efforts were true and sensible but I failed to execute at the right time. As usual, like every day I logged on my laptop, checked news on streaming and one bottom line of the news injected a small shock for a moment-Delhi Mayur Vihar? Interesting, I pushed the volume up and got a very paining answer, 'If guys can play with our feelings then why can't we?' was the consensus. What in the name of holy mother Mary; look at the nerve! I felt a sharp pain in the gut as a number of depressing questions arose. I racked my brain to remember the details again. She is also from Delhi. What did she say? I laughed and then grinned as I realized, I couldn't remember anything except the echoing giggles. It was hard to curb the urge. I had to confirm if she is a trustworthy, innocent, & straightforward girl as I had reckoned her to be. However, what would I ask her again? I just had to wait for a while before I found out a reason to call her. I was choked when I heard that. When she chided me, I abused myself on acting like a dork. I thought, she knew how to tackle a guy.

'What were you doing?' I asked and made a guess that she was in metro.

'Nothing,' she answered and added, 'Hey, I'm in yellow line, network isn't proper here. Will call you when I'll reach Kashmiri Gate.'

I replied, approaching to water bottle on the table, 'Ok, sure.'

I didn't know how far Kashmiri Gate was form Rajiv Chowk (CP) as I never visited Delhi before. So I was counting minutes in wait for her ping. After half an hour, my phone flashed arrival of her message, 'Hey, I'm with my cousins, talk to you later.' Eyebrows pressed together, up in the centre, I felt bad as she told me that she'd call and now...Delhi girls. Rather than being human, I called her shamelessly; she picked the call and asked, 'What were you doing?'

'I just came from the class,' I answered.

'Then why don't you take some rest? We can catch up later,' she urged. I was too eager to talk her. 'Are you busy?' I asked. She said very cutely, 'No, just with my cousins.'

'Ok, you enjoy with your cousins.'

'Okay bye,' she disconnected. How clever they are? God what you put in these girls when they were in mother's tummy, I murmured.

Message For You

D for Delhi and D for Dilwale but she was not
such a Dilwali.

There is difference between love and like. You can like anyone even if
that person isn't physically present but love only happens when two
eyes meet and dream together. I started liking her but it wasn't love and
I wasn't in hurry to fall in love with her because still somewhere it was
just a conversation which didn't have a strong foundation to carry any
relation. You can't carry any relation if it doesn't have any future and we
didn't have any future so I was just happy with this unnamed relationship.
We just had one week talking over the phone. I messaged her simple
good night message and within a minute, got the same reply from her
end, I smiled and that was enough to make me sleep happily, considering
it an indication that someone cares for you. How stupid I was?

We Indian guys have always been sensitive because still we have
role models like SRK from Kuch Kuch Hota Hai and Dilwale Dulhania
Le Jayenge. One more reason could be that they're being pacified by
the media and specially by girls who tell them it's okay to cry, you just
need to find the real man in you.

She just replied with a general civic sense in today's gadget-world,
whatever it was, it was the first message between us, which I saved in
draft and became memorable message, how sweet, and how stupid it
was.

The days were normal but the nights were too cold, next morning, when I was rolling in my cozy bed, unexpectedly my phone rang with arrival of her call, I charged up. Clock said 8:20 am. I answered her call. She replied with a cheerful voice, her voice chocolaty that I liked most to make my day, 'Hey good morning!'

'Good morning,' I replied, deliberately groggy.

She suddenly said, 'Are you sleeping? Get up now, aren't you heading for college?'

'I'll, it's only 8:20 am. I have forty more minutes before class begins,' I covered myself in blanket in the cold morning.

'Forty minutes before class begins and you're still in bed?' she screeched.

'Yes,' I said proudly, coming more close to microphone as I wanted to hug the moment in my bed, shrank in bed.

'Get up now.'

'Bah. Okay. 10 minutes,' I said warily and wanted her to order me to get up.

'Sir, get up. It's not good for health to sleep like this, okay,' she said. I snorted.

'Argh! Get up means get up,' she repeated. It feels special when someone wakes you up early in the morning and you give all the reasons not to wake up.

'Yeah good night bye,' I moved my fingers to cut the call.

'Wait! Okay listen. Come in your balcony now,' she said as she is the most innocent girl I had ever met. When a girl acts innocently, there must be a reason behind. I was shocked.

'What?' I was awakening now.

'Anuj, I said come in your balcony,' Pakhi ordered, seemed as we knew each other from so long. I walked towards balcony. The cold wind rushed towards me, a feeling of cold gentle bliss that a splash of cold water could never give. I breathed deeply.

'Okay. I'm in the balcony. What now?' I asked feverishly.

'Now dance,' she said and burst out laughing.

'Ah! How can you do this to me?'

Still laughing, 'How do you feel in this winter?' The wind poked every cell it could. I was shivering. However, felt something different and why not, this happened first time with me, yes, first time I woke up so early.

'Yes very warm, thank you.'

'I was just kidding, Anuj. Now get ready for classes.'

I sighed, said 'Ok', and hung up. I walked and almost jumped with ecstasy, the energy had nothing to do with the fresh air. I rolled in the bed again, hugged pillow and closed my eyes for few seconds, it was pleasant to sleep in last ten minutes, always like heaven. Last ten minutes are always most important, either it's before examination or waking up early morning.

I was ten minutes late for my class. I entered in the lecture theatre; Prof. Mahajan was taking lecture on stable and unstable systems. I was completely unstable the moment I reached in the class. Physically I was present in the class but mentally I was in daydreams, dreams with bird of desires. Suddenly I found him in front of me and asking the question about essential conditions for stability.

'Now I am gone,' I thought for a moment. Complete silence in the theatre, I looked at him, as he was expecting something from me and nothing came out from my mouth. I took some time to recover and gave the answer confidently. I felt relaxed when he said, ok sit down and be in class. The class had been overfed for a shock. After five minutes of refreshment break, I was ready for the second battle, entered in the lecture theatre and decided that I wouldn't repeat the same thing again.

Unexpectedly in the second class, nothing changed and I found Prof. Mohanty said, 'You roll no. 20, are you in class or somewhere else? Get out of the class!'

He didn't even give me chance to answer any question. I thought I could answer and be in class.

'Sir, I was just…,' I tried to speak.

He repeated, 'Get out of the class.' I felt ashamed, came out from the class.

'What's wrong with me…?' I came and lay in my bed and just opened the lid of my laptop, browsed Facebook and sent a message to her. A girl can change your life, this fact I had just realized. Things were changing in life, especially in lecture theatres. My friends used to use Reliance CDMA for talking to their girlfriend. They were in relationship but I wasn't but I tried to get it in few days else it was difficult for me to manage with recharge coupons.

Bizarrely I asked her in the evening, 'Hey can you manage a reliance phone. So I can call you.'

She replied glibly, 'Hey, but this is fine, what's the problem with this?' Is there any problem?'

'No, it's ok,' I responded but didn't know it was difficult to manage two in pocket money meant for one. She didn't stop there and added, 'Moreover couples use it and we are just friends.' This was the last bullet to take my breath. I had no other reasons to make her agree for Reliance CDMA. I stood up, took some water and replied, 'Okay fine, no problem.'

We became part of my daily schedule and good friends. I started putting my phone on silent or vibration all the time. Even in the class, my fingers were on keypad and eyes on the white board, this is how I managed the love engineering.

Every day was different from the previous one and I got to know something about us. Girls are the best creature of god but they are the unpredictable creature to hide all the secrets of them. Call duration was inversely proportional to my monthly expenses, and my wallet was getting lighter now.

When you step out for education or to make your career, you have two options, either you can fly and count the beer bottles, or you can follow a decent path of life. Who didn't want to fly but I had chosen and followed the decent path because I had seen my father working late night at office when I was a child. They never said No and I never asked for more, whatever they gave, I managed with that only and obviously, that was enough for me. *Now with money for one, I was managing two...*

Oops! More Than That

When things come on your head then you realize its importance and impact. Many times life gives these many situations to go through it, like when a prince comes out from his home to learn the lessons of life, or a naughtiest girl becomes mother and takes all the responsibilities of her child or a hip-hop guy becomes father and take responsibilities of his family and their prosperities.

One day she called me and we talked for more than half an hour, suddenly the call disconnected. I called back and asked, 'What happened?' She said despondently, 'Balance over.' This was the best time to hit the iron and cash the opportunity.

'I have reliance phone, if you can manage, then we can talk freely,' crossed my figure, shrugged my shoulder, I asked, indispensable.

She replied sombrely, 'I don't have but my cousin uses, so I can manage but I'm not sure.'

'No problem,' I took a long breath, relaxed…smiled…happy. The mission was accomplished. Though our eyes didn't meet yet but our feelings somewhere met in clouds via satellite. We were connected 24*7.

When a girl lives alone, she has so many things to share because every day she has to face life with all the twists and turns and especially Delhi girls are chatter box. She started sharing her naughty ideas, her problems, stupid talks and many things which we were not supposed to discuss but we did. It's good to go with the flow if it's not sex. While

21

having sex you need to stop for precautions' else we could contribute more to increase the population of this country. If she had a problem, I had solution for that.

When we are away from our home and family, we need people to share our feelings. If we get the right one, we carry them till the seven vows.

It's very important how you look at any relation. In college, we spend all the years just to know our marital status but you shouldn't run to know or to change your marital status, you can just feel and enjoy the unnamed relation.

I too didn't want to know where this conversation was going. I was just true from my side and was ready to be the same for years for her. She was staying away from her family living at her uncle's home, so, many times, she missed her family. I could feel myself as her true friend. I knew how difficult was to not miss your home, that too when you are papa's best daughter. Sometimes tears wet my cheeks when she used to open her old memories. Everyone has a past, some people have good memories and some have good lessons. She never wanted to go away from her family but when her father had gone through paralysis attack, her elder brother sent her to her uncle's place for further studies.

It seemed like she got everything in just few days. She just needed a friend who could listen to her and now she had the best one. Though I was supporting her but I wasn't superman. I was just few months elder than her. It's always great when two immature ideas take a mature decision. These were just our feelings which were marrying with each other, mixed and made a wonderful shake to taste it. How a mamma's boy became a responsible person, I couldn't realize.

One day suddenly she called me, 'I don't want to talk to mamma, and everybody hates me.'

'Nobody hates you Pakhi,' I replied glibly and listened everything and continued, 'Mamma was just giving you suggestions, right or wrong, why you are feeling like crying, I am always with you okay,' I replied poignantly and she cried at the next moment. I knew her very well at times and felt that something was hidden and untold. Her moods swings confused me. Something happened in her life before but I never asked as I didn't want to make her sad, I just made her realize that she was the best girl in the world. Nobody is perfect in the world; you just have to make them feel their importance and perfection.

'Hey Pakhi, you are the best girl that I know, I just want something in return,' I used to say.

'What do you want from me?' she usually replied.

'I can have your hug which is priceless for me.'

'Shut up, you are a mad guy.'

I tried to make her happy, my crazy talks and her stupid replies, we were not aware but somewhere we were making new memories. We were making the GOLDEN NEST of our friendship, true, deep and strong and crazy of course.

'Would you always be my friend?'

'No, I can't promise.'

'Then get lost.'

We used to laugh. Good sense of humour is important to know about a person, to handle and to make your different identity from others. Sitting with aunties and mother actually, I could try and understand girls and their feelings – what they like, how they think and what they feel. She was childish; she was dependent, careless and a lot more. She used to forget to have milk in the morning, never had anything before sleeping and I always shouted.

'Early in the morning, how can I have a glass of milk and sandwich?'

'People eat much in the morning, so that they can work for the day. Have, else we won't talk,' and my play card always worked. She used to warm me and that after coming from college, she would take revenge of it and I was always ready to be punished by singing her favourite song.

She messaged me that day, when she was on the way to college. Pakhi:

```
I don't need heaven. I just want to be with you
as a good friend. My feelings are true. We are
very good friends. I want to prove those people
wrong who say; a boy and a girl can't be good
friends.
```

Me:

```
I am always with you and now you can enjoy your
life because it will never comeback.
```

That day, I promised myself, I'd be her best friend forever, no matter how I handle her because it's always difficult to handle a girl and especially when she is far away from you.

Marital Status: Single, Committed or Complicated?

When a girl comes in life, there are certain things which surely happen like, waking up early morning just to check, if you miss any message or call to respond from your phone which is always on vibration mode, looking at the mirror whenever you get time, even a pimple gives you so much tension more than any assignments to submit next day or taking all the suggestions for your each step you take in life. It was dawn when I woke up at 5 pm because I had to wake up late night to talk to her.

'Hey Anuj! Come, let's play cricket, don't sleep so much,' I was standing in the balcony when my friend shouted from the ground floor.

'I just woke up, you guys carry on,' I replied, rubbing my eyes and yawning, went inside and again fell on the bed; shoved my hand under the pillow, took the cell phone out and messaged her, 'Hi.'

Practice makes a man perfect, my fingers didn't need looking at keypad even, and they had a good practice to run with half closed eyes and this I learnt in the class when my eyes were on the white board and fingers on the keypad of the phone.

Stomach on the bed, one hand on the right cheek, my phone flashed, arrival of her message-

```
Hey! I told you my friend Prateek is coming to
meet me today, so I met him in afternoon, that's
why I couldn't call you.
```

25

Prateek was her school friend who was doing engineering from Jaypee Institute of Information Technology, Noida. When it's about some other guy, you get all the attention. I replied at the next moment, 'Hey! How are you?' Rather than replying to my message, she called me. I picked her call, 'I am fine, I enjoyed a lot today,' Happiness was in her voice and with her crystal clear voice she added, 'I met Prateek today, and he was looking so cool.'

Usually problems start from this only- *We enjoyed the whole day with him and he was looking so cool.* I didn't speak over it. I felt jealous and it verified that I was a human with emotions and feelings. I was biting the bullets as she was describing the things about him. It's not only love but other relationships also which you don't want to share with anyone else.

'And you know I told him about you,' she said.

I interrupted in between, 'What did you tell him about me?' I wanted to know was that good or bad, of course I didn't want to compromise with my image in front of anyone being her best friend.

'He called me fatty. Am I fat…?' She asked and couldn't complete her last sentence.

'No, you aren't,' I replied though I didn't meet her yet. Now I got confused. Is she fat? Moreover, if yes, then how much, it was funny but took my attention for a while.

'Anuj, she is your friend, doesn't matter she is fat or slim,' I picked an apple from the table and gave a hard bite on it.

'I am very happy today,' she broke my silence.

'Why?' I asked, rolling in my bed with an apple and ate few more bites.

'Prateek proposed me today,' she said and everything paused for some time. I was shocked, left the half-eaten apple and sat on the bed.

'What?' I asked again surprisingly with unfinished bite of apple inside mouth.

'Yes, Prateek proposed me today,' she repeated the same line with the same tone.

'Do you love Prateek?' question came out from my mouth, wiping my mouth, I asked without thinking anything.

'I don't know but we are very good friends from last few years. Now he's doing engineering, he's intelligent, and cool too, so...' she didn't complete her sentence. Unspoken words are always dangerous. The last word of her line was the reason of my all questions.

'So...?' I asked without patience.

'I didn't accept his proposal but I think I'll be happy with him,' she shot the bullet in my heart.

'Do you love him?' I asked in hurry. I just wanted to hear a negative reply from her.

'Don't know,' she replied with confusion in her answer. I disconnected the phone-line.

We were very close friends now. Our day started together and ended with the same. I was happy and she was enjoying it. This wasn't love but I was scared to leave her. She started calling me but I didn't pick her call. After an iteration of calls, my phone beeped with her message.

Pakhi:

```
Please pick my call. Please once pick my call
where are you Please Anuj once pick my call.
```

I answered her call with a question, 'You love Prateek?'

'What happened?' She asked.

'I don't want to lose you...,' tears came out form my eyes and wet my cheeks and then lips.

'How can you do this with me, why didn't you tell me earlier, why? I don't want to talk to you now, please leave me alone.'

'I don't love him, I was just kidding, and you please don't cry Anuj.'

'Don't lie, you love Prateek, he proposed you, you said, you are my good friend but why didn't you tell me even', I asked, I rubbed my face on pillow and wiped tears.

'It's not like that, I don't love him. I was just kidding. Trust me,' Pakhi replied.

'I am your friend, right, then please don't cry and listen to me, it's nothing like that, it was just a joke,' she pampered me as I was her baby.

'Prateek suggested me this stupid idea to check. He said that you love me,' she dropped some ice cubes on my burning heart. 'Feeling jealous, ahem,' she added.

'I can't talk to you like this,' I raised my voice and allowed my anger to come out.

'What happened?' her voice low, she seemed uncomfortable and helpless.

'Nothing; I'll talk to you later,' I said, before I disconnected the call, she started pleading, 'You won't disconnect the phone line, okay.'

When you get some importance, you become a king and feel that you are the only person, so I disconnected.

Alternatively, both the phones started ringing. I wanted to pick and talk, but sometimes you have to go away to come closer. I kept my phone on silent. Cell phone started beeping arrival of her messages.

Pakhi:

```
I was kidding; I'm really sorry, if I hurt
you... I didn't mean that
```

Pakhi:

```
Please trust me, please pick my call.
```

Pakhi:

```
At least talk to me. Please once pick my call.
Please.
```

Pakhi:

```
Please just once, please.
```

Nevertheless, I picked her call and we clarified all misunderstanding and things came on the track. Things were not broken; those were forming with strong bonding.

'I was joking and made a whole drama of it. I'm really sorry, if I hurt you but I didn't mean that,' she said. It seemed she had wet eyes too.

Most of the times when girls hurt they have one sentence to say-*I'm sorry if you are hurt but I didn't mean to hurt.*

'It's ok, I just don't want to share you with anyone else. I don't want to lose you,' I sniffed.

'I'll never give you any chance to lose me,' she promised. We roasted our friendship with more affection, care and dedication for each other. Where this friendship was going, for a moment, I just thought?

What would happen after college, just like other relationships?

You are Far, but Near my Heart

Happy days go with rabbit but sad with tortoise. She was going to her home for a week. Now it's going to be difficult to talk to her at home.

'Don't miss me too much. I'll come after a week. I have promised you so many times, now it's my turn, promise me you won't skip your dinner, breakfast and lunch,' she said, and wetness in her voice as she didn't want to go. I wasn't happy with her departure, and ended it with, '*Hmm,* but don't repeat my lines, I should tell you that don't miss me.' I could feel her emotions at the very next moment.

My eyes were wet too, 'Hey what happened?' I asked.

'I'll miss you.' her words floated into tears.

'I know but don't cry. You are going home, so just chill,' I came close to the microphone and added few PJs that always made her happy.

'Have fun as much as you can, eat and don't think much about your figure, we'll manage later,' I laughed. I knew that seven days were going to be without fun, joy, happiness and naughtiness. I was going to miss her badly. Next morning she had to leave and got a message in the morning-

```
I am leaving, please don't cry, you study
properly for your exams. You have to score well
and don't miss me. Be with your friends and come
late in your room okay. I'll really miss you,
take care.
```

Those days, I never missed any class and didn't give any chance to any of the professors to kick me out of the class because that was the best place to spend time and not to miss her. Sometimes you involve with few things which help in other ways.

It was just a third morning when I was waiting her to come online on G-talk. A message popped-up on the right side of my laptop screen.

Pakhi: Hie :)

Me: Hi, I was waiting for you from last one hour :(

Me: How are you?

Pakhi: I was with mamma. I'm fine. How are you? Did you have your breakfast?

Me:I am fine :(

Pakhi: Missing me?

Me: No.

Pakhi: Swear on me?

Girls always have tendency to listen what they want to listen. I couldn't control my feelings saying that I was missing her badly.

Me: I miss you a lot :(When will you come back?

Pakhi: On Wednesday

Me: Come soon. Can't you come before Wednesday?

Pakhi: I will come with brother on Wednesday. You spend time with your friends, you won't miss me, and how was your exam.

She changed the topic and asked about my exams and I understood she is also missing me a lot.

Me: Fine.....but that wasn't exam, that was only a test and it was fine.

She didn't understand why I typed 'Fine....' I was more specific with dots.

Pakhi: Hm

Her reply 'Hm' calcified that she had no answer. Girls always type 'Hm' when they are not sure, when they are confused.

Me: Well you say how are your days going with family?

Pakhi: Awesome, bindass:) All time I just eat and sleep. Mamma was just saying, why I carry books if I don't need to study. LOL

Me: That's great. You enjoy your days but study too.

Chat message popped up,

Pakhi: Don't be my mom please ;)

Me: I'm not kidding; you have enough time to study then you should not waste.

Pakhi: Hm, I'll.

'Hm' means, what'll happen, who knows.

Me: Promise?

Pakhi: promissssss

Her reply with multiple Ss again certified that she was not going to do what I said.

Me: Miss you :(

Pakhi: Miss you too

Me: Come soon.

Pakhi: Mom is calling

Me: Go…breakfast time, I know you have to say something!!!

Pakhi: Hey, not now. Some other day, I'll.

Me: Okay now go, mom is calling.

Pakhi: Miss you a lot. Take care, bye.

Me: Miss you too, are you there?

Pakhi is now offline. Pakhi will see this message when Pakhi comes online.

She said she has something to say to me, though not right away, I thought. Maybe she loves me too and is waiting for the right time. Or did she mean to say she is missing me at home.

'Of course, she doesn't love me. How can anyone love over a phone,' I concluded this and left. I was staring that green mark which was gray now-*offline*. I stood up but once again I sat back just to check the status, if she could come online again. I went to the conversation history, and went through whole conversation again. I felt good by doing this. I composed a mail for her, expecting that next day she'd read it-

```
I miss you with every beat of my heart, I don't
know why. You are the only one for whom I think
a lot, you are the one for whom I cry and you
are the one who make me smile :( I'm missing you
badly. Come soon. Take care.
```

It's always tough to spend time alone when it never happened before. Time heals everything but how much time that we never know. This was all happening with me first time and every day was new, brighter and happier than other. I was just waiting for her to come back.

She came back to Delhi after a week and the worst time had come to answer those questions that we never expected to come in the question paper. Knowledge matters, marks don't matter but why parents don't understand this. The boy, who used to sit on the student's desk in the class, was actually sitting on the teacher's chair in the hostel. Yes, being an engineering student, it was my responsibility to teach her mathematics because she was from medical background and in her life sciences course there were few subjects of mathematics.

This is our education system. One side our government talks about progress and other side they don't even know what to teach and how to teach. Even in one of the toughest exams IIT-JEE and its prestigious IIT campuses, we still have old syllabus. If medical students are supposed to study mathematics in medical then why were they not taught mathematics in school days, and if there is no need to study mathematics in medical then why have subject of it in syllabus. It's like; you cut the legs and expect the person to win the race. I wish I could directly map votes to the wishes of people of our country. Get the vote, only if you fulfil the wishes of citizen. We still study about those devices which don't even exist now or are not in use, but to get the degree you have to follow the rules and regulations of our Indian Education System.

I could sense exam phobia in her voice as Pakhi said, 'I'm from bio background, I haven't studied Mathematics except in 10th standard, how I'll score in examinations. I'll go through only few chapters; I just have to pass this exam.'

'If you try with me, there won't be any problem to score at least seventy five percent,' she started laughing.

'Seventy five percent in mathematics, are you joking? That's not my cup of tea engineer; I just want thirty three passing score, that's my dream for this year.'

'It's not like that', I assured her.

'I don't know what is Integration, Differentiation, how'll I score?'

Being confident, looking at laptop-calendar, I assured, 'You don't need to worry about Mathematics, Electronics and Physics, I can teach you and you start Chemistry and Biology, even I can guide you in Chemistry too.'

All the chemistry of life happens with Chemistry classes. I could spend more time by teaching her these subjects.

I smiled, 'You have to work hard with me. We can do that.'

'Without fun, life is none…' she cracked a joke.

'Nothing can work for you,' we both laughed added, 'but we need to score well.'

'More than 75, right?' she laughed aloud.

'Not kidding, okay. If you score well then it will really help you for your higher studies. And who knows, tomorrow, I'm with you or not but you'll feel proud of me,' I laughed.

'Nautanki…if you'll go anywhere, I'll come there with you without asking you even,' she made me smile and little emotional.

'Sure?'

I tried my best and applied all management skills to manage that notorious girl. Glibly, I used to shout at her, but that worked every time. We had to run with Ferrari to win the race.

'I am able to do this Anuj.'

'Pakhi, it's not about exams, we score or not, I want you to give your hundred percent, after that if we fail, nobody will say anything to you. At least we can give our best.'

'What did aunty eat when she gave you birth?' she laughed.

'P-A-K-H-I…'

'Okay, sorry. I will do that. Now let me study, then we will talk.'

When I cared, I cared like a mother and listened as a father, when she shared her secrets, she shared as a sister and when she cried, I was always there to pamper her. We were not making any new definitions of life, friendship and dedication, we just lived the way we both wanted to live and made a new era. She was being dependent on me and that I never wanted to make her do. I wanted to make her independent flying girl who wanted to live with her dreams that she dreamt but never discussed with anyone.

```
Tere liye toh har hadd se gujar jata,
Ek baar tere labon ko mauke toh dete.
```

Image0179.jpg

When it comes to all your reputation, it actually matters how you manage the things, how you handle the things and how you make someone comfortable with your company.

In Indian every second girl believes that every person who has white skin and a good build is best for her. We don't accept that fact but that's the reality. If you don't fall into that category you are above them.

It's difficult for a boy to make her realize that he is best for her. What are the skills you should have to be the best partner?

1. You should be very understanding and have to give her some space to fly and let her explore the world.

2. Fun Loving – Seriousness is not the solution for everything when it comes to love, life, family and friendship. There are many problems in life which can be resolved happily but we cry and do it. That doesn't affect much but if you do it with smiles, it gives a sweet aroma of life to be with your partner for rest of the whole life without any obligations.

3. Good sense of humor – Now time has changed; you can't just sit and love your partner with all day dreams. No, you just need to be very practical. Making someone happy in a relationship is not just that easy. You need to be creative. Being romantic is good but you need to be creatively

romantic. Buying a card from Archies and gifting someone may be romantic but making a card and then gifting, can make a big impact, and needs effort to do that. The amount of effort you put in your work, you just need a very little part of effort in your life. We actually miss these small things and then we say- *things are changed now; those were different days when we used to enjoy a lot.* Romance is not a job to do but it's less than. It needs effort and you have to do it and then see how magically it works to make your life happy again.

4. You should respect each member of her family- Every person deserves respect, no matter they are your in-laws. In-laws are as sweet as our family members, only Ekta Kapoor has showed them bad. If you give respect, you get respect. If you make difference, you will feel the same.

5. You should respect her wishes and dreams- Every bird is made to fly, you can't just cut feathers just to make sure that someone doesn't fly (sounds better). Every person has dreams and you should respect them. May be two people have different goals and dreams but they are equally important for both of them.

6. Be a caring person- You should care for her because she is yours, if you won't care then who else will come, still if you think you shouldn't, there are many others to care for her, then you don't need to regret.

I was well aware with this. Recalling these terms, conditions and precautions, I was heading to have dinner at mess. She called me, 'Hey where are you, my result is out.'

'You didn't check?' I asked very eagerly.

'No...'

'Wait I'll just check,' I replied. I was more excited to know. I was sure for her good result but scared with the word result. I turned to the hostel and just browsed www.du.ac.in and entered her roll number 4046417. I was shocked when her result flashed out there. I didn't believe for a moment but I had to accept the reality. I called her at the next moment, 'Did you check?'

'No, you told you are checking, what happened, did you check that?' she seemed scared.

'Were your exams not good,' I asked her, still looking at the screen and started adding marks of all her subjects to calculate the percentage.

'What happened?' she asked with the same tone in shock.

'No, nothing, it's fine,' I replied.

'Anuj, please, have I not passed,' she asked in hurry.

'No, you passed,' my voice was low and I wanted to tell her the truth but I didn't else she won't be able to control her emotions.

'What happened?' she asked again.

'Nothing.'

'Anuj speak up.'

I replied her with a very low tone, 'You have scored seventy percent.'

'What the F...,' she could only speak this.

'Are you serious?' she didn't believe that she scored so well.

'Seventy percent,' we both shouted together.

'Yes we did,' I could feel her jumping on the floor at the other end.

After few days when she got her mark-sheet, she scored 78 in Mathematics, second highest in the class. We live for these moments in life. Making someone smile or feel special gives a special feeling, and at that time, there is no other thing to think about.

```
How can I forget those days? When I sang songs
for you,
How can I forget those days? When you slept with
my songs,
My voice was your strength,
```

```
Your presence was enough for me,
How can I forget those days? When you enjoyed
within me
```

Day was special and now I wanted to make it more special. I wanted to see her, at least her photograph because there were not many photographs on Facebook and any photograph looks good on Facebook, I wanted to see the real one. Like the other day, she didn't come online that day. I called her just to know the reason. She picked my call, 'Who says, I don't study, I have scored seventy percent,' she came out from her cave.

'What happened, why are you so excited?' I cracked a joke.

'I have scored seventy percent, top ten in the class,' she said very proudly.

'Yes, because you are intelligent,' I smiled and felt good because she was going to give all the credit to me.

'Don't laugh Anuj Tiwari, I had tequila shots,' she replied, her tongue slipped.

'Are you drunk?' I didn't expect her to drink and then she was talking.

'Yes, I want to live my life, Paro wants to fly my Devdas, Paro wants to fly,' she was completely drunk. I didn't have words to reply.

'Sunita are you there?' she asked.

'Yes, I am here only, are you drunk?' I didn't feel comfortable with her voice now.

'Sunita, you are my very good friend, you are my best teacher, you taught me, I shouted many times but you didn't say even a single word, Sunita, today this Paro is going to fly …'

'Pakhi, talk to me properly,' I said.

'Paro will fly today, don't stop me today I won't listen to you,' she was not able to speak properly. Hope I could be there and slap her hard. What the hell, she was drunk.

'Hm…where did you drink?' I asked without any kindness, actually rude this time.

'With you,' she started laughing aloud and added, 'I didn't drink.'

'I'll kill you.'

'Were you shocked?' Pakhi asked, still laughing and giggling.

'Of course not,' I replied.

'No Devdas no…,' with her melodious voice she was flying with happiness.

'You have gone made.'

'Where are you?' she asked.

'As usual, that bridge only,' I replied.

'Oh, on Love-Bridge,' excitedly she asked and added, 'then sing a song for me.'

'No…'

That bridge had so many stories. So many love stories started with that place and our was the first exception that our friendship was cherished there.

'Please, I want to listen,' she requested.

'You go and drink,' I teased her.

'Fine, never talk to me.'

There was complete silence and that was the perfect place to get someone's dreams and wishes fulfilled. She asked, 'Are you there?'

```
Tu Hai Aasmaan Main, Teri Yeh Zameen Hai,
Tu Jo Hai To Sab Kuch Hai, Na Koi Kami Hai,
Tu Hi Dil Hai, Tu Hi Jaan Bhi Hai
Tu Khushi Hai Aasra Bhi Hai…
Teri Chaahat Zindagi Hai
Tu Mohabbat Tu Aashiqui Hai Tu Aashiqui Hai…
```

'Are you there,' I asked, taking a long breath. There was complete silence as before I started singing. I repeated again, 'You there?'

After few seconds, she sniffed, 'Never leave me, you are my best friend.'

'Hey, what happened,' I pampered her as she became emotional.

'From the day you came into my life, I feel good, I shout and you never say even a single word, you are the best,' she started crying. I didn't speak anything just understood the life of a girl when she is away from her family. She needed a guy in her life as a friend and I never wanted to break this friendship.

'Hey, come here, don't cry, mad girl you are, I'm always with you,' I held her emotions, coming close to microphone. I could feel her presence. When you have strong feelings for someone, distance doesn't matter. She was far away from me, but not even a single day she slept alone. She always slept with my stories and songs.

```
You are near, far too.
You are my happiness and smile too.
You are peace of my heart and excitement too.
You are my world; you are my life, and everything
you are.
```

When she slept I started finishing up my work browsing some analysis on Google. Google always plays a very important role in life. If your wife is angry, just google it, if you are looking for some fun, just google it. There is no confusion to say that there should be degree given to google as well once engineering completes.

A pop up message appeared on the right bottom side of the screen. While those links were processing, I clicked on pop up message. It was was Pakhi.

Pakhi: Hie :)

Me: Hi :) you didn't sleep?

Pakhi: Ninni aa rahi hai.

Me: I knew that. Good, you leave your exams and sleep, don't study. Let's sleep bye and don't call.

Pakhi: What happened, just for 5 minutes :(don't log off, just 10 minutes talk to me ok?

Pakhi: Let's chat for some time on net then I'll study and you'll teach me.

Me: If you are not sleeping then can I see your photo?

There are few things you should never ask, age of a girl, her weight, her photograph and her figure. Anything if you ask, take at your own risk.

Pakhi: Why?

Me: I want to see.

Pakhi: Nooooo.

Her 'Nooooo' with five Os, I understood that there might be possibilities to see her photograph.

Me: Why? I want to see, we have been talking for more than a month.

Pakhi: So what?

It was more than a month since we were talking and I had a right to see her photograph but she didn't understand that and not showing photograph to me made me anxious and curious to know the reason behind the way she wrote 'so what'.

Me: I'm not kidding.

Pakhi: I don't have any photograph.

A Delhi college girl doesn't have photograph and specially the best one, was not believable. There was something wrong; a cold chill ran in my mind to know what that is.

Me: Don't lie ok, you have.

Pakhi: But that's not good.

Me: So what, that's yours, that's fine.

Pakhi: That's very old.

Me: I'm waiting.

Pakhi: hmmm

Me: ???

Are you there?

Pakhi: Wait

100% excited, but 50% scared. Excited to see her for the first time and scared if she is not beautiful as I expected from her voice. Does it matter? Not actually, but sometimes. As her voice was melodious, so my heart made a beautiful image of her in my mind and started dreaming. We were just friends but still. My 50% fear was enough to make my excitement 0% but chances were very less, I logged into G-mail simultaneously, refreshed page multiple times. After a while I received an e-mail from m......16cool@gmail.com with a subject. :)

I clicked on image0179.jpg. 50% fear was 0% now, 100% excitement was also 0% but happiness was 200%.

Smile on my face, mouth corners pointed in the different direction.

'Not bad,' I said in the air. She looked healthy but cute. I looked at the mirror, 'She is your friend not your girlfriend, and it's a very old photograph.' I saved that photograph in C drive so no-one could see that. I replied her with a smiley.

Me: Thankuuuuuuu :)

Pakhi: Happy :)

Me: Thanku :) not bad it's k.

Pakhi: Hmm

Me: It's good, you are smart. hahaha

Pakhi: Ya, but girls are pretty not smart ;)...dumbo

Pakhi: Howz that???

Three times question marks were forcing me to talk about her photograph.

Me: Wait…System is scanning image0179.jpg ….system found few viruses.

Pakhi: System found which viruses? Mr. Antivirus???

Me: System found…Nose is big, face is tilted, and eyes are very small.

Pakhi: Anything else :(

Me: Just kidding, looking good, thankuuuuu :)

Pakhi: Why, thankuuu ?

Me: My wish ;)

Now get up and study.

Pakhi: Now you are with me, I'll pass with good marks in others as well.

Me: But you should study? I can only help you.

Pakhi: Hmm

Girls' 'Hmm' means absolute 'No'

Me: Get up ok.

Pakhi: kkkkkkkkk

Her reply with multiple Ks means perfect lie.

Pakhi: Now you show yours.

Me: How can I show mine……hahahaha?

I laughed aloud, naughty thoughts in my mind. We were very good friends and sometimes we had discussed the things which were not supposed to be discussed between a boy and a girl but we did.

Pakhi: *Chata khana hai?* Show me your photograph, please.

I wanted to mail my few photographs, dragged few to desktop. I chose the latest one of my college. I wanted to edit those in Picasa but I preferred to send the original only but later on, I realized I could make it cooler.

I wanted to have a sip of her excitement so I replied with N O with many Os.

'Nooooo,' I replied, copying those photographs in a folder named My_photograph.

'Please...Please...Please,' Pakhi requested in a loop as generator started.

'No...No...No,' in a same tone, same manner, I replied.

'Ok, fine byeeeee,' she showed her childishness.

'You angry...Hehehe...Wait,' I pampered her.

I uploaded photographs on G-talk. I knew that the next question would be 'Can you mail me your photograph?'

'I can see you there but can you mail me?' She questioned at the next moment.

'I don't give my photograph to strangers,' I whispered, came close to microphone.

'Okieeeeeeeeeee,' she said and silent.

'First you mail me at least 100 photographs of yours,' I asked and tried to make her naughty.

'Nice joke...I don't have now, I'll click then I'll send you ok, now please send me your photographs, else I'll not talk to you,' she seemed serious this time but again lied that she won't talk to me.

'I have already sent you, you can check your mail,' I replied, clicking on the sent items.

'Fully packed photograph,' she laughed.

'I am in the jacket, this photograph is eight months old, well how's that?' I asked expecting positive reply from the other end.

'Not bad, hehehehe. I mean it's good,' she replied. Truth comes at the first go so I wasn't sure, she liked it or not.

'I am not motu like you,' I asked, laughed but actually wanted to know, does she really look fat or that was her old photograph.'

'Am I motu?,' she replied and questioned back to me.

'No my baby, you are the thinnest girl of the world, right na?' I cracked a joke, stood up, and stretched my body as much as I could.

She yawned. I said again, lying in my bed, 'Now we have to study, get up, it's enough for today, come on come on....get up and no ninni now.'

'Okieee...give me two hours, I'll be back soon, Pakhi will be back soon,' she said very confidently.

'Bie, take care and keep water bottle with you, whenever you feel like sleeping, have some water or wash your face,' I took pillow and laid in the bed again.

'Okie.....Byeeee.'

Call disconnected.

Don't Go Home

Any place where we can remain, or at least become completely relaxed physiologically, psychologically and mentally is called a home. No, there are certain other things as well that you need to remember. You have to wake up early in the morning, no matter you have reasons or no reasons to wake up so early.

Don't even forget to inform your mother if you are going out, else there are fewer chances you would enter home happily. Your cell phone can't ring too many times else there would be series of questions you need to answer. Lastly you can't get a new haircut. After all these obligations, legalities and limitations, it's always a home. It's a place where you live your whole life just in few moments without any blink of sadness, that's called home.

There is special feeling when your father shouts at your new haircut, he doesn't feel bad actually to look at your new look, but he just wants to see you at the next level of life. You are questioned when your cell phone rings all the time, it is a known fact that you must be having a girlfriend or a boyfriend, but a mother just asks to know who is that person. More so because she can't see you heartbroken and crying later on.

She shouts when you are late, but keeping glitters in her sight, she serves food late night, just to feed, as she used to feed when you were a kid. The only difference is that at that time you were kid, and now you are grown up but feelings are the same as they were.

Father pulls your sheet up to wake you early morning not because he doesn't want you to sleep but he wants you to be healthy and lead the world. A father always has dreams that he couldn't fulfil in his life. His eyes always see dreams in yours every morning.

Mamma called me early morning, 'All the best my beta, today is your last exam.'

'Yes mamma but this is just an exam, don't worry,' I replied.

'Now get up and have your breakfast, it's five.'

'Mamma, it's 4:50 not five.'

'Beta you'll get late, get up,' she repeated and added, 'When are you leaving, today or tomorrow morning?' I didn't reply because I didn't plan when to leave for home. I took my reliance phone to call Pakhi, looked at it, I already had three missed calls.

'What happened?, mamma asked.

'I have to study. I have to score good marks, right? So talk to you later, bye,' I replied. Pakhi was already on call on other phone.

'Ok beta all the best.'

'Thank you mamma.'

'I have to study. I have to score good marks, right? So talk to you later, bye, you liar,' with giggles, she started laughing.

'Yes, I'll score well,' I smiled too.

'Ok, now you study, call me once you are back, I need to talk something important.' Call disconnected and I left for exam.

There is always someone special who wishes you before you leave for any important work. She was the one for me. Didn't matter if she was busy she would call me just to wish me. I didn't believe in wishes and prayer but there was always a support and faith that worked well.

When I was back after the exam, the first question she asked was when I was going home. She always became emotional whenever I had to go home because after going home, we could never talk as we used to.

I replied, 'I am going in the evening.'

'Good, you enjoy your holidays with your family, happy holidays,' she replied. If you're well aware of Indian culture, it's the easiest job to know about a girl and her feelings.

'You also enjoy your holidays', I said.

'Hmm,' Pakhi replied, low voice.

'Oh really…hmm; I'm just kidding. I'm not going today', I said and waited to hear her happiness from her words.

'You are not kidding me,' she asked surprisingly.

'Yes, I'm not kidding.'

'Sacchi…,' still she didn't believe that I wanted to stay just to talk to her for the whole night.

'Mucchi, I am not going today.'

'But tomorrow you will go,' her words expressed the bonding we had made in the last few months.

'Let's not think what will happen tomorrow, can we spend good time today?'

'Sure, sure, philosopher,' she was happy now and made me smile too.

That night we both didn't sleep, eyes were red but still bright, phone was almost burning but still I could feel her fragrance, we were far away but still together, connected forever with a thread of life, friendship and dedication.

Next day I had to leave. I came outside to LB (Love-Bridge), perfect silence, birds were chattering, sun was red and growing slowly-slowly; wind was blowing and touching my cheecks and as I felt, whispered into my ears, 'You are going to miss her badly.'

I asked her, 'Will you miss me Pakhi?'

'Nooo…'

'Hmm me too…' I teased her. The moment I said *me too* she responded, 'Of course I'll miss you, who will teach me? Who will wake me up for studies? Who will remind me for breakfast, lunch and dinner? Who will sing songs for me? Who will make me happy when I'll feel alone? Who will make me cry when I'll not care for you?'

My eyes became wet and tears came out at the next moment but those drops were giving me a pleasant coldness when it flowed from eyes to lips, at the last, gently left the chin and then collapsed. A drop of tear is so much valuable when someone cares for you and we did for each other.

'Don't miss me, we'll talk…don't worry,' I said over the call. She interrupted, 'But not like this, we will not be able to talk like this I know.'

'We'll talk like this only, I'll not give you any chance to miss me,' I felt a gust of vacuum in my stomach as I lost something for a moment. I was actually afraid, why, didn't know.

'I promise you but you also promise me that you'll have your breakfast, lunch and dinner properly and most irresponsible thing when you study, you don't keep water bottle with you and then doctor gives you tablets of dehydration. So please take care of yourself. You have stomach infection so please don't eat outside,' I added.

'I am not a kid. Go and talk to me every day and I don't want that you disconnect my call, so please pick once I call you.'

I knew that she didn't want to leave me for a single moment. Our lives were like black and white picture, when we were together we just filled colors in it.

```
Sometimes…JOKER…sometimes…SINGER…sometimes…HER
HERO…EVERYTHING I was. When she used to wake
up, I welcomed her with my smile. Whenever she
felt alone, I switched on my webcam and made
her room noisy. Whenever she felt bored, I even
danced in front of webcam, how crazy I was but
I was happy to be like that.
```

I didn't give her any chance to miss me. It was tough but manageable. We used to talk till late night. Sometimes my mamma caught me talking to someone putting pillow on my head in the bed. That time I had to pretend, 'No mom, just listening songs.' There is nothing without risk and I was ready to give anything in return to get her presence around me. Not everything but few things are surly fine in love and war.

I was just waiting for her birthday on 30th May which was the first birthday with me, and I had prepared a long speech for her just to speak over the call. However the way is always tough when destination is not less than a dream. Dad wasn't well and I was giving head massage and keeping wet cotton on his forehead. Being the son of the family it was my responsibility and my habit too which I inherited from my father.

I dropped her the message at 11:59, a minute before so it could take a minute to deliver, and she could receive at sharp 12:00 because I wanted to be the first person to wish her. Message said-

```
Hey, I remember the day well, 15th Feb, morning
7:50am; when I talked to you. Now I can feel the
sense why did that happen. Wish you very happy
birthday. I don't have much to write, only few
words that I am happy with you and want to keep
you smiling and happy forever. Today we have
completed 104 days of our amity and I hope,
we'll score many centuries like this.

You are not my alarm watch but I always wake up
with your loving voice.
You are not in my family but I feel you are a
part of it.
You are not in my bookcase but you guide me like
a sacred book.
```

You are not here but I can feel your presence
around me.
I am always there for you because I have a
friend like you.
Enjoy your life in the whole sky.
Live as much as you want, go and fly.

A Journey to Remember

When you are away from something, you know the value of it. Moreover who would know how it felt to be at home for a guy like me who never wanted to go away from his family. Though I had a best pal in my life but I always enjoyed my days at my home in Bareilly. I was coming back to home after meeting Sharma aunty as she invited me for lunch and asked thousand questions about career after engineering. I could only answer the best one about an IT job. My cell phone vibrated, I parked the bike and it was Pakhi. I picked her call happily. It always makes us happy when we get unexpected call from loved ones.

'Hey, how are you?' cheerfully I asked her.

'Did you tell Maddy about us?' she asked without speaking anything else. I didn't get what she wanted to ask.

'You told Maddy about me. You and Maddy are planning to make fun of me. How can you do this Anuj? Don't call me ever. I'm going to change my number. I got you; you're a cheap guy who was playing with my feelings from last few months. I can't believe you can do this to me. Never call me. I was stupid who talked to you.'

I couldn't even understand what she was talking about and it made me crazy. I was shocked, 'what happened, tell me, what are you saying, I'm not getting?'

'Don't lie. I know everything now, you are a crummy guy, better stop talking to me, else I'll change my number, just get lost from my life.'

'Please trust me, I didn't do anything, please tell me what happened,' I asked in hurry before she could disconnect. I just felt nothing but helpless.

She disconnected. I called her many times but she didn't pick and if she picked she wasn't ready to listen to me. The worst I could do was to abuse Maddy as much as I could. I understand that Maddy had poked his nose in my life. An actor can't direct the movie or a director can't act in the movie, didn't matter how smart I was but when it came on me, I didn't know how to handle the situation. Only thing I knew that after walking so far with her I never wanted to turn back. I decided to go to Delhi to meet her. I never imagined that our first meeting would be like this. These thoughts only could give fire to my anger and Maddy was lucky that he wasn't in front of me.

I reached home and told my mother that I had some urgent work at Jaypee Noida which was one of the branches of Jaypee group of institutions.

'But suddenly…,' she queried.

'Mom, it's really urgent, I'll come tomorrow, I have to go regarding college work else they'll stop my placement,' I replied and crossed my finger.

Next day early morning, I boarded train from Bareilly to New Delhi and reached there at 9:30 am.

My dad always used to remind me to keep wallet in the front pocket whenever I left for college. First time I forgot, and Delhi proved that to rob in front of cop is easy. When I de-boarded the train, I had lost my wallet. Everything was there in the wallet but now I had nothing, just a note of twenty-rupee in my pocket, which I had kept in my pocket after buying the water bottle.

'What should I do? Should I meet station master but what will he do?'

'Should I inform dad?'

'If I inform him, first he'll shout and then he'll call my friends at college and that is going to be a big mess.'

I skipped all the rubbish ideas and I dialled my friend's number who was in Noida at his home.

'Hi aunty, this is Anuj, Shubham's friend. May I talk to him?' I asked her and calculated how much money I'd require to reach at his place.

'Beta he is out of station, tomorrow he'll come back,' she said and I disconnected saying thanks to her. Life is not sweet every time and especially my life was on a different track from yesterday. Drowning man catches at straw. One of my old friends was living in Noida Sec-62 but his number wasn't reachable. I just regretted not maintaining any communication with him. Why repent now, when the bird has already eaten the crop. I had many friends but when I looked for them, not even one I could find. I understood I had to face this anyhow. I sat for some time as my throat was dried up and my eyes were almost full with water. I kept on calling Pakhi but she didn't pick my call. When there was nothing to think, I just started walking. I was thirsty now but I preferred to drink that salty water at the station rather than buying water bottle. Just in few moments, I understood very well how poor survive.

'I walked for few minutes and tried to take lift but I was not a girl so nobody looked at me,' I abused every single person who just passed by in car or bike. I had to walk nine kilometres and that I completed in two hours.

How difficult a friendship can be, I never thought but I had hope that whatever I was doing, I'd get results of it. I was sure, she would talk to me and things will get resolved.

It was early June. The whole NCR was burning, and finally I spent those twenty rupees to buy a water bottle. Those few sips of water,

I could never forget in my life ever. It was actually A JOURNEY TO REMEMBER, a journey which made me realize the meaning of life, dedication and friendship.

Somehow, I reached Jaggi's home. My skin was tanned and face looked like that of a caveman who hadn't taken a wash in days. The moment I knocked his door, he was shocked. Only one thing made it easy that his mom was not at home.

'Hey what happened to you Anuj?' he just couldn't understand what to say. He took me inside and I sat on the sofa.

'Hey, nothing and sorry I have come without prior information,' I had no other option but to say this.

'It's perfectly fine my friend. I am so happy to meet you after years but I didn't expect to see you like this,' he just smiled looking at me. Before I took bath, I explained few things to him as to why suddenly I reached there but not completely as we were meeting after years.

I called her again and again expecting that she'll pick once after getting frustrated and I could tell her that I had come to meet her.

'What happened Anuj, please don't call me,' she repeated her words in anger without listening mine. Jaggi's mom entered while I was calling her standing in the balcony.

'Who is he?' she asked Jaggi.

'To whom is he talking?' she asked him again.

'I don't know,' I could hear Jaggi's reply to his mother and then tried to hide my face in frustration. I was helpless and tired too. When after sometime I couldn't bear it, I started calling her madly and just told her, 'I know you don't want to talk to me but I have come to Delhi just to meet you, may I come to meet you?'

'I don't want to meet you Anuj, I told you, and I don't want to talk to you. Why are you calling me again and again,' she replied very rudely. For that moment, I abused myself to be the biggest loser. Jaggi's mom looked at me once again but I pretended that I was talking to my mom.

I begged her, 'Please just once, I want to meet you.'

'You didn't ask me before coming to Delhi, so go back, I don't want to meet you,' she replied with the same tone, same anger, nothing changed. If something changed, that was my face, my feelings and my eyes which were full of tears now. My body was sweating, face was red, head was burning and I was in pain.

'Why are you talking like this, please I want to meet you, I'll clear all your doubts, just once, at least give me a chance to explain myself,' I just pleaded this time.

'Do whatever you feel like but I can't meet, it's better you go back', she said very angrily and disconnected the call.

After that moment I just wanted to call Maddy and abuse that asshole but there was no point when she was not ready to listen to me. Jaggi said, 'Hey Anuj let's have breakfast.'

'Yeah coming,' I tilted my head towards the room to hide my tears. For a moment, I felt regret that why I had come, I lied to my mom too. I closed my eyes and tears came out. I felt bad that a girl who cried for me, made me cry. I washed my face and felt empty inside my heart. I just messaged her-

```
I am not wrong Pakhi, I know time isn't with me,
but I'm not a cheap guy. I trust and respect
you. You have misunderstood. Please trust me.
I miss you.
```

A U-Turn

Things just changed in two days. It was dusk when I was packing my bag to come back home from Delhi; my cell phone rang. It was Anushka who was a good friend but we hadn't met from a long time as we both were busy with our lives. She was my cousin Kavya's best friend. I remember the first time I met Anushka. She was gorging wildly on a hot dog in a restaurant, and I had laughed at her loudly. Though I am still made to pay for that but that is a fair price in exchange for a friend like her. Shiny long honey-coloured hair, rosy red luscious lips, a heart-shaped face and her luminous blue eyes had always held my attention. Her wide mouth and the adorable dimples on her cheeks, her naughty but charming expressions always won the hearts of others. Pronounced cheekbones, a stunning smile, and long eyelashes—she was beautiful. She became a very good friend of mine and she was my naughtiest friend. She was from a Punjabi family. *Punjabi girls always rock*, she used to say to me. We had spent a good deal of time roaming around in the lanes of Connaught Place in Delhi. At times, her caring nature confused me. Her respect for me and the way she supported me in difficult situations made me wonder if she loved me. Friendship had a very different meaning for her and that was, in fact, more pleasant and truer than love. Therefore I say—*Punjabi hearts always rock...and Punjabi kudiyan always hot*.

'Hey, this is Anushka. How are you? Where are you, and how's life?' she asked me.

'How did she come to know about it,' I thought for a moment and answered, 'I'm fine, just came to Delhi for some work.'

'Work?' she pretended to be shocked and added, 'Kid has grown up now. See you at CP tomorrow evening.'

'Hey I have train in the evening. Let's meet in the morning at 11,' I said.

'Sure, will give you a call,' she was happy to meet me but I wasn't in a mood to meet anyone. We talked for next few minutes about studies and all and left few things to talk about tomorrow.

Next day we both met at CCD, CP. We started opening threads of those days when we used to meet and roam around in Delhi in summer vacations. She asked me about college and asked what work I had in Delhi. I didn't want to lie as I had already lied to my mom and what results I got in return.

'How long have you guys been dating?' very excitedly she asked me.

'It's nothing like that. We are not in relationship, we are just friends.'

'Did you meet her?' she questioned me in confusion.

'No.'

'Never?' shockingly she looked at me holding coffee in her hand.

I nodded, 'Yes.' I explained everything how we started talking but I didn't expect the end that I got. I didn't want to discuss with anyone anymore.

'You have come to Delhi because she is angry. Cool,' she took one more sip of coffee and looked happy, confused and then smiled. I nodded again.

'Do you love her?' she asked expecting that I'd say yes.

'No, we aren't in relationship,' I said.

'You are not into relationship and you have come to Delhi to meet her because she is angry. Is this not a dream?'

I just smiled and said, 'I wanted to clear her doubt because I was blamed for few wrong things.'

'That's all perfectly well but let me clear a few things with you. Do you like her?'

'Yes, I do.'

'Do you love her?' she asked at the next moment, putting the cup on the table. I couldn't answer this. I just started thinking about the day when I started talking to her and this day when everything seemed over.

'Do you love her?' she asked again and pushed the coffee cup to my side a bit.

'I don't know.'

'If this is not love then what? You guys are talking from last four months and everything was just perfect. She is angry and you have come here to meet her, what is that?'

'I don't know but now everything seems over Anushka,' I looked at the other side. I didn't want to lose Pakhi. I had come so far and going back wasn't an option. I wanted to try to make things normal.

'Hold on Anuj, things are fine. Don't run, just give her some time. Things will be fine for sure,' she held my hand which was unexpected. She looked into my eyes, smiled and released her hand.

'If she didn't want to meet why did you come here?' she asked casually.

'I wanted to give her surprise,' I replied, holding cup in my hand.

'R-O-M-E-O...Oh God,' she laughed and reminded me of a few things that my mom used to say.

```
We all are human and we all have emotions. If we
expect something from someone and if we get that
then we are so happy and keep that person in
```

our heart forever but when we don't get what we want, we become hopeless and unhappy. It's like if we expect 90 percent from someone and get only 80 percent, we aren't satisfied and feel bad. From the same person if we expect nothing or less or let's say 50, and that time if we get 80, we feel so happy and cheerful because we got more than we expected. In both the cases we got the same which was according to our deeds but the only difference is of happiness and sadness. The things I can conclude from your words, you are a nice guy for any girl who looks for true love, care, dedication and friendship. And I am saying, this is just love, nothing else, so just love her.

'Hey, thanks a lot. Now I am fine,' I said.

'Now come with me and we'll have pani puri,' she pulled my hands and we roamed around.

I just kept on thinking about her words that this is love, and I love her. In the evening I came back to my home. Feelings always overrule anything and our bonds weren't so weak. I knew Pakhi will call, and I was eagerly waiting for that moment.

'Is this love?' many times I thought, many times I fought with my heart but the answer was same, 'You are a liar, whatever is happening is love not friendship. If it's friendship then what is that when you wake up early in the morning for her, when you care for her more than you do for yourself, and what is that when you sing songs for her, and give her best sleep. Have you ever done the same for your friends?' I was in love with her but wasn't sure about her.

I got a call from her, just after three days and she started crying over the call.

'What happened?' I asked.

'I'm sorry. I shouted at you without any mistake of yours. I know I troubled you a lot. It won't happen again. Please forgive me. I am so sorry,' she realized that I didn't do anything. I was happy that a third person couldn't break our bond. Our bond was tested and we came out stronger.

'I just want to say, I won't lie. I won't hurt you ever. You can trust me,' I said and felt happy. I wanted to ask her if did she loved me but it was too early to ask as we just came over an emotional break.

June passed with tears and smile, July passed with laughter and August passed by writing new memories of our friendship and dedication which was growing. I was confused and still unused. When I say unused, it means that my lips were still dry, my dreams were still full of action movies rather than romantic or rom-com movies. Nevertheless, one thing was clear in my mind, a boy and a girl can't be good friends, if they are then I was not one of those saints who just wait, wait and wait.

Finally I smiled looking at the mirror, and accepted that I was in love.

Half Girlfriend
with Full Feelings

'How to propose a girl?'

'How to propose a girl over phone?'

'What are the best ways to propose a girl over phone?'

I started searching the best way to propose. No matter how smart you are but when you have to face it, then it's the real test of your skills. I was not best but creative enough to give surprises and romantic too. However, I was not getting the best idea to propose her. Technology can't defeat emotions and I preferred to be real and raw as I was till now.

'No need to show off, just switch off the lights and propose to her,' my heart said. This time my mind supported my heart and I felt goosebumps...smiled...laughed...crazy...mad...*aashiq*.

'You really love her? Or this is just an attraction?'

'I am in love with her,' my heart replied with a sweet smile.

'If she'll refuse then?' stupid mind asked.

'No answer...perfect silence in my romantic heart.'

'But I am sure, she'll not refuse, she talks to me till late night. She cares for me, she knows me and she cried for me that day, that means she has feelings for me,' my heart gave the perfect answer and mind countered smartly, 'That's the problem you guys have. If a girl talks to you properly then she loves you, if a girl cares for you then she loves you, what the fuck happened to you. You both haven't met each other, how can you say that she loves you. May be she loves you but still at least a meeting is important to fall in love officially.' I was stuck now because I had all the reasons to accept what I just thought.

Though we were talking in the same way but my feelings were changed for her. I was in love with her and it took me one more month. September had come and it was 6th September '09. From last one month, I was just thinking about her as my love and she was talking to me as best friend. Things were on a different track and I had to make it come on the same. I felt goose bumps, smiled, laughed, mad, *aashiq*.

I jumped on my bed, took cell phone, and dialled her number at the next moment. She picked the call after few rings, 'Hello.' 'Hi, what's up?' I asked, took a long breath. She could feel something unusual as my voice was changed.

She replied in confusion, 'Nothing, you say, what's going on?'

'Nothing,' I replied with a low voice, still scratching the table with my nails. Same place, same table where few months ago Maddy dialled her number.

Before I spoke anything, she asked, 'What happened Anuj, is everything okay?'

'Yeah, everything is fine,' I replied, rubbing my fingers. I tore the paper into pieces and pieces and pieces.

'Why are you talking like this, I'm your friend right, what happened, tell me, want to say something?' she asked again.

Though care was in her lines but 'I'm your friend right' made me uncomfortable and whatever courage I had gathered to speak went in vain. It's not too easy to tell someone you love her. It's as difficult as you wish for your dreams to come true. As usual at the right time, my mind gave me wrong signal, 'Reality always exists behind the camera and you haven't met her so it's better to live in reality else it's just

ᵗ⁄ Without meeting her you are going to propose to her?'

'You there?' she asked.

'Yes, sorry, nothing, yes I am here only.'

'Just finish whatever you are doing we'll talk later. You seem busy.' She seemed frustrated.

'I with call you in five minutes.'

'Ok.'

Call disconnected. The moment the call got disconnected, I didn't listen to anything because the more you listen, more you get stuck. We should always listen to our soul's advice only. I called her.

'Hey what happened, tell me.'

'Your net is working? I have some work; my net is not working,'

'Yes tell me, should I log on my laptop.'

'No, it's ok, I'll try once again, talk to you later.'

'You are such a dick stupid guy,' neither my heart nor my mind supported me.

It was tough to say that but somewhere I was scared to lose my best friend. A friend can't be your love and love can't be your friend, that's the fact. I wanted to tell her that I was in love with her but I didn't want to lose anyone after saying these words. I took few sips of water and called her for the last time, 'I want to talk to you.' She understood that something has happened, 'Wait I'm coming in my room, just hold on.' The hold-time made me uncomfortable again but this time it was do or be an asshole.

'Are you hiding something, tell me what happened, is everything ok?' her voice showed her confusion and she guessed something happened.

'Everything is okay; was feeling alone so I wanted to talk.'

'Who's saying you should feel alone, I'm always with you. Did you have dinner?'

Darkness made me comfortable to tell though it was stupid but I did switch off all the lights.

'I love you…'

It was silence for a moment. 'What?' she said.

'I love you…'

When you feel helpless, even non-living things give you courage. I held the chair tightly, I replied, 'I am not kidding, I love you.'

'Anuj! I'll kill you,' she treated my words as a joke.

'I love you, I'm not kidding.'

'What are you saying, we are friends,' her voice grunted for a while but cleared later on.

'I don't know but I really love you,' emotions, feelings, courage, everything in my voice, wiping sweat from my forehead. In the month of September I was sweating profusely, that was enough to express my situation. Being a courageous guy, I said once again, 'Pakhi! I love you. I wanted to tell you this thing earlier but couldn't say. I want to be with you forever.'

'You haven't seen me Anuj. How can you say this?'

'That doesn't matter for me,' I replied very confidently. I thought either she would say yes or diplomatically no but she started crying.

'Hey, why are you crying?' I asked her.

She sniffed, 'I never thought about this, I don't want to lose you Anuj.'

'I also don't want to lose you. I'm waiting for your reply.'

'If I'll not reply, will you leave me? I don't want to leave you, you are my best friend, and I never thought about this, why did all this happen?' the way she was saying all this, I was concerned about her happiness first.

'Hey, please stop crying.'

'Will you leave me?' she questioned as she was afraid of losing me.

'I am not going to leave you. You are my good baby? So please stop crying and have water,' I pampered her.

'But never leave me alone, I'll not be able to manage,' she didn't answer my question but her tears showed how strong our friendship was.

'I promise you, I'll never leave you, it's my promise. Now get up and have some water.' Proposal was on hold and it continued. Girls take time to accept proposal that I knew but it was more than four months. I was with my half girlfriend but with full feelings and months passed expecting that she'd say yes soon.

Stunning Place
with a Cute Face

Finally we planned to meet in Delhi. I was excited but scared. I was happy but nervous. I was in the seventh heaven but how to react, that made me nervous every time when I thought about it- what will happen when we'll meet.

Girls are considered the shyest creatures when it comes to marriage, love making or public romance. This is a myth that girls feel shy when it comes to taking decisions about their future. Scenario has changed now in cities where people are educated or from educated families. Girls are very much independent and able to break the weird tag of male domination. At the other end guys are more shy and are very sensitive about things or people or relationships. Now they have tendency to face more, suffer more and cry more alone. A crying person doesn't define weakness; it defines how much sensitive, caring and responsible he is. This may seem false but that's the fact.

Only one can rule and now girls have started ruling. These all thought made me more nervous though we were talking since last more than 10 months. It usually happens, guys can't express their feelings easily and this strongly proved that I was a complete man material.

I had never visited Delhi before. The things I knew were described by her only. If I knew anything about Delhi, it was Delhi girls. Delhi girls are the prettiest girls across the country. Not only are they best in dressing sense but very much cool the way they talk. Their faces show how much open attitude they carry towards life, which is supposed to be lived. There is no doubt if they are secured, they can make Delhi the new Bollywood. Moreover I was excited to meet my dream girl. Delhi was chilling at its peak in December as usual *Delhi ki sardi.*

'Are you coming tomorrow?' excited, happy and with honeyed voice she asked.

'I can't come, I am really sorry. Don't worry; we'll meet next month for sure. I was just about to call you that mom isn't well,' I informed her, entering my room.

'What happened to her?' her voice changed in deep sorrow.

'She isn't well and wants me to stay at home.'

'So you are not coming,' she asked again.

'I'm sorry.'

I could only say this and disconnected the call.

'This is your pickle, your biscuits, your *Besan ke laddoo* and rest of the things are in your bag, check it again,' mom pointed to all those stuff.

'Mom, please, nobody will have all this except your magical *aam ka aachar* and *besan ke laddoo.*'

'Shut up, this is for you, keep it there and sleep. Tomorrow, early morning you have to leave,' mom shouted putting other stuff in the bag. I checked her gifts again and of course I was going to meet her tomorrow. There is no happiness without sorrow and I just wanted to make her realize that.

Love makes you a liar. I told my mom that I was going to my college, and in a way, yes I was going to college, just after a small *love break at Delhi* which was going to be the best memorable day of my life.

Next day early morning, I boarded the train from Bareilly to New Delhi, intercity express. I just loved getting window seat. Window seat…earphones…high volume, and I started my journey… JOURNEY OF TWO HEARTS.

'Today I'm going to meet her who was only in my dreams till now.

'I love you Pakhi,' I murmured and smiled looking outside the window. I woke up from my utopia, suddenly a baby shouted, 'Hey mom, Coww…close the window….she'll come inside.'

I looked at that baby girl; she was cute, sweet and innocent. She looked at me and smiled. I blinked my eyes; she jumped on the other side of the window.

'Sweetie, come here,' her mom tried to catch her.

'Hehehe….heeehehee…' baby girl just laughed, looked at me.

'Mommy…C for Cat or C for Cow, tell me mommy, tell mommy,' baby girl pulled her mom's hand and swung all around.

Her mom looked at me, 'She is very naughty.'

I grinned, 'But she is very cute, what's her name?'

'My name is Zafira, and *dady mujhe betu bulate hain.*'

I laughed out loud, 'Hahaha…Thankyou so much Zafira.'

Things look beautiful and people love you so much when you are in love, I felt the same. 'What's your name?' baby girl asked looking at me.

I smiled, 'My name is Anuj.'

'Tell me your full name, I told you my full name na,' putting her hands on the seat.

'Oh sorry, my name is Anuj Tiwari,' I pinched on her cheeks.

I wanted to tell her that I met someone like her but this was going to be a surprise visit so I didn't call her. I just logged on my laptop, opened the folder 'Win32' and browsed few of her photographs. When you expect, it never happens, when you don't it always does. It happened with me. My cell phone rang, 'Hi, *kya kar rahe ho aap,*' she asked me.

'Nothing I'm out with mom, will call you later,' I informed her.

'Okay, let me know once you are free.' Call disconnected. One message flashed on the screen —

```
'Anuj Tiwari always tries to give me surprises
but every time I catch him. This time once again
I caught you. I know you from last eleven months.
Early in the morning, "I am out with my mom"
lol…dumboooo :P'
```

I called her up the next moment.

'You liar, I knew you are coming, why were you doing this?'

'I was trying to give you a surprise.'

'And I caught you,' she laughed.

'I tried my best. Now you have to pay for this.' I added, 'What's going on?'

'Nothing waiting for you…come soon…'

'I'm coming, be ready to meet me.'

'Excited?' asked she.

'Are you excited?' I wanted to know her reaction.

'Obviously I am. Let me meet that guy who has been talking to me from last eleven months. Let's see who he is actually.'

```
I love the way you are, I love the way you talk,
I love the way you are.
```

We planned to meet at CP metro station. Cell phone rang, 'Where are you?' she asked.

'Just reaching CP, where are you?' I asked, looking at the route chart in the metro as CP was just next station from New Delhi.

'I am waiting here at CP.'

Everything was happening in blinks and I was just reminding myself what to say, how to speak and how to act well like a gentleman. An announcement happened- *Next station is Rajiv Chowk, doors will open on the left. Agla station Rajiv Chowk hai darwaje bayin oar khulenge.*

Hiding my face in the metro, I slapped on my cheeks three four times just to look fresh. Someone looked at me, before she could change her perception I stopped. Door opened, someone pushed me as they all started the race or as if a flood came from the back. I came out with them. I was conscious for my each footstep. I looked around me and wished that I could see her first.

'Does it really matter? Yes of course.' I thought. She called me and I informed her that I was standing near CCD.

I looked at a girl in extra makeup but that suited her. She was not just good looking but stunning and gorgeous but I crossed my fingers and wished she wasn't Pakhi.

'I am happy with my cool girl; I don't want any hot girl, they are tough to handle.'

She approached towards me and just crossed. I took a breath and looked around waiting for Pakhi. I stepped close towards CCD. Some weird questions started coming into my head.

'What if she isn't as cute as she appeared in the photographs?'

'What if she smiles in a weird way?'

'What if she is not good?'

I blinked my eyes and asked myself, 'You love her Anuj?'

'A lot…I am ready to live rest of my life with her.'

'Then go ahead and accept her as she is, because happiness matters at the end of the day, not physical beauty,' I smiled and became happy.

'Hi.' So polite, so soft, someone said from behind. I turned back.

'Hi.' I could only smile.

Oval face, black eyes, curved shaped eyelashes, eyebrows shaped like a bow, giving perfect contrast to her complexion. Chocolate color lip-gloss on her pink lips, her lips were like pulp of a flower. Her untied hair fell on her cheeks with a gust of wind. She was wearing blue-chocolate colored sweater, earphones in her ears, fish shaped earrings that hypnotized me for a moment, red cheeks, a cute face. She looked like a baby girl. But I looked at her as my soul-mate, her body appeared so perfect, so young, so poised…COMBO PACK… BABY AND BEBO, I smiled.

I wanted to look at her from top to bottom; very slowly, I did so. She looked at me; I turned my sight and then body to the other side. Anxious, shivering, my heart beats ran with horses. I tried to behave as if I was relaxed and cool but reality was inside my heart, I was nervous. She smiled that tried to override my senses. Silence between us made me more nervous. We didn't talk much and exited the station.

Taking the long circle, we went to the other CCD. I pushed my footsteps back. She was one-step ahead now. I looked at her from the back.

'She isn't only cute but hot also,' my mind punched on my heart.

'Anuj! Shut up, she is your love, don't think all these rubbish things,' looking downwards in shame, I ignored.

I planned many things; first, I'll shake hands then a proper smile and then we will talk and I'll ask her few questions but nothing happened.

She asked, glances to the left during speech, 'What happened?'

I synchronized my steps with her, went ahead a bit, 'Nothing.' And then something happened...

First Touch & Seven Messages

She seemed shy and silent. Obviously, her state of mind wasn't different from mine. On phone, we talked for three hours per day but from last thirty minutes we hardly talked for more than ten minutes. We reached CCD. We were trying to ignore to look into each other's eyes. I wanted to tell her many things but...how, that was the question. She picked the menu. I got the best time to look at her when she was looking at the menu, though I couldn't see her face but I could feel her. I wanted to stop the watch.

Suddenly she asked, looking at me, 'What do you want?'

I just turned my eyes to the other side. I was sure she understood that I was looking at her from last few minutes. I looked into her eyes for a while. So beautiful and they said many things. There was something special in them.

'Whatever you like, you can order,' I replied, turned my eyes and again looked into her eyes.

'Okay I'll order, one brownie and two coffees,' she grinned.

'Okay,' I grinned too.

'Why didn't she order only one coffee, so that I could have a sip on the same place where she touched her lips.' I imagined.

We took some time to get comfortable and then started talking. After having few sips of coffee, she took something out of her bag saying, 'Hey this is for you.'

'Is this a ring?' I thought.

'Such a dick you are, would she buy a ring for you or would you get for her?' and I got the answer next moment itself. Then I expected a love letter.

She kept a diary on the table and started showing pages of it. On the first page, she wrote something in italic letters '2friends+2gether=4ever', on the other pages there were four cartoons. Those all targeted me only. One was just browsing photographs on the laptop, second was making a squared face as I always did when she didn't pick my call, third one, a guy was crying, holding phone in his hands, and the last one was a guy talking over phone in bed as I used to do, actually we both did.

I looked at her and smiled.

'How is this one?' putting her finger on the angry face, she laughed. She cleaned her lips from tongue.

'Not bad. Is this for me?' taking that in my hand, I turned the page of the diary, next page said-

```
Hi,

I am your diary. I'm here so that you can
share anything with me, good or bad, anything.
Treat me as your mirror from which you can't
hide anything. But before you start, I want a
promise, that you will not scrap even a single
page of this especially for phone numbers or for
your any stupid work. Hope I'll always be with
you as a thodi khatti and thodi meethi memory.

All the Best for your future.


YOUR DIARY!!!
```

The moment she gave me that diary, I had decided to write each moment of us in the diary. I didn't know what and how would I write but after writing everything I'd gift it to her when we'll get married. We were not in a relationship even and I planned till marriage, love is all about that.

Now it was the time to prove myself as the most romantic guy. I unzipped my black colored Nike bag and picked one pink color heart shaped card, which I made for her.

'Hey, who made this,' Pakhi asked, snatching from my hand.

'For you,' I replied, looking at her fish shaped earrings, which were touching her neck as if they were kissing on her neck again and again. I held her hand into mine. She forced herself not to look at me, and then I held her hand with both my hands.

I picked up the heart-shaped card, put that on the table and pushed it in front of her eyes that were still staring somewhere else. She looked at that pink handmade heart-shaped card and then looked at me. She picked it up. It said:

```
You always make me feel that I don't need
anybody,
Since the day I talked to you.
```

I held her hand in mine and said, 'Every night I missed you and every night I just tried to know why I'm here because you were not with me that time.'

I put the second card on the table, very softly and with all the love. She took it and that said:

```
I love to wake you up early in the morning
because your voice makes my day and your laugh
fills happiness in my life, and when I talk to
you, I forget everything.
```

She looked at me as I continued, 'Every night I slept with my tears. Each and every moment was hard to live and your absence made me helpless.'

I brought out the third card and it said:

```
After talking to you for so long,
I again wait for the next moment to talk to you
What is that, I don't know but something special
I feel.
When I call you again and again, you shout, but
I miss you...
But I love the way you shout and then care for
me, I just love that.
And yes…your smile after a big fight, I lose my
heart all over again…
I don't know what magic it is but I love this.
```

I didn't say anything this time and just picked up the fourth one and put that on the table and few drops of tears dropped on the table. The fourth one said:

```
Many times, we fought, many times we shouted,
but after that always you made me cry because I
missed you a lot,
I am sorry but don't fight, talk to me,
I miss you a lot, when you don't talk.
```

Teardrops were continuously wetting the table and this time a drop of tear dropped on the fifth card, which said:

```
I just love to pamper you, care for you but I
feel bad when you cry alone.
```

The fifth card made her eyes more wet, she kissed on that teardrop which dropped on the card, 'You are mad,' she wiped her tears too.

'I don't want to say anything.' I put the sixth card in front of her and the sixth said:

```
You are the best girl I've ever seen, whenever we
talk over the phone, there is always a thought
in my mind that I love you so much...
```

'If you think, you should go for the seventh card, which is not as simple as the other ones; I hope you'll accept from your heart whatever I've written in that. Should I give it to you?'

'Give me the last one,' she tried to take it from my hand. I gave her the seventh card:

```
I just want to spend rest of my life with you...I
love you.
```

'These lines are just for you,' I said, took a sip of coffee, poured more love in my eyes.' I said. 'You are a mad guy,' she smiled, shook her head and then grinned. I looked at her intense eyes and made a guess that she was thinking about me. You shouldn't force someone to fall in love with you, you should just love. I did the same. She didn't reply whether she accepted my proposal or not.

'I have something delicious for you,' I picked the box out of the bag.

'*Besan ke laddoo,*' she took the box from me and added, 'I just love it, thank you so much, you are so sweet. No, say thanks to aunty,' her happiness gave me pleasure and her eyes forced me to love her more. 'I can give you one, if you wish,' she smiled.

'Haha…no no you have,' I laughed.

She kept those cards in her bag and happiness I could see on her face but what had to happen more? She still didn't accept my proposal…

```
The way you are, makes me crazier TO LOVE YOU
more.
```

Kissed Without Permission

What really happens when you go for movie with a girl? May be you go, watch movie with snacks and come back. But what happens when you go for movie with a girl whom you love so much? I didn't want to predict because it was unpredictable enough for me to go for a movie at the first meet when she said, 'Let's go for a movie'. We reached CSM mall, Noida Sector 18. Looking at the pamphlet, I asked her, 'Which movie?'

She replied, '3 idiots.'

Two lovers are going to watch 3 idiots, I smiled inside.

'Let me get the tickets,' I said and approached the ticker counter.

There are some manners which we studied in adult moral science of college which said-

- A guy can't be late if they both are meeting; else he has to pay big amount for his mistake. Girls can keep that excuse till the time you hold a stick to walk.
- A girl shouldn't get up to take the order when you are sitting at restaurant or food court area. Nowadays that has been changed because girls have becomes more particular about diets. So this can be tentative.
- A girl shouldn't buy drinks for you, no matters how big or small person you are, guy is made to love her not to make her walk for you all the time.

- You can always trust on girls' choices and you should, because they have best sense of social appearance for you. You just can't wear anything in front of them.
- Only a girl can make you human from animal, so believe in her suggestions. They will wake you up early morning to go for gym, or can help you to take critical decisions about your work and any social activity.

These are the certain things which nobody can ignore about girls. I just wanted to make these things official but still my proposal was on hold and that made me conscious. I reached at the counter.

'Should I ask for corner seats, that was the question?'

My heart said, 'You love her and she loves you, then of course corner seats will make you both comfortable and couples usually get corner seats. Go ahead.'

My stupid mind, 'Who says she loves you, she didn't say I love you, did she? So don't live in dreams, being a decent guy get the seats in center.'

I just asked the counter lady, 'Two tickets, 3 idiots, 1:10 show.'

'Two tickets sir?'

'Yes,' I said, giving 500 rupee note.

'Ok sir, two tickets, sixth row from the back,' lady replied, giving tickets in my hand.

'Thanks.' I took this tickets and left the counter. I-2, I-3 it was. I visualized I-1, 1-2, I-3 and then other aisle?

'How sweet you are. You help people to make relationships,' I wished for that ticket counter girl. I considered it was in my luck.

Happily we entered. She looked the seats but didn't speak so it wasn't a big deal to think too much. Only few questions were still floating in my mind.

'Is she your girlfriend? And if not then what's going on now?'

'I am not doing anything…IT'S HAPPENING,' I smiled. I-1 was not occupied and we seated on I-2, I-3. These were the corner seats, actually the wall corner. I smiled again with few goose bumps. Movie started.

'Does she love me or not, if not then why are we here?' I asked myself.

She looked so gorgeous in the theatre, more beautiful at every next moment, light from the screen on her face seemed like we were under moon light. I clicked those moments in my eyes forever and saved them in my heart to tell our kids that HOW I MET YOUR MOTHER. I looked at her small fingers and tried to touch them. She looked at me, 'It's good na,' she asked, showing her nail-paint. I got embarrassed, for next 15 minutes, I couldn't try to move from my place. She was enjoying and I was lost in her.

This is completely a female dominating society, I just concluded that. But I wanted to live with them.

I felt something cold, pleasant touch on my hand. She held my hand and looked into my eyes. I didn't know what happened suddenly, I was just hypnotized? First time, I actually felt why love is blind. There are few moments in life which come for blinks and if you think too much, they go away and then there is nothing except regret; It could do that. So it's better to cash the opportunity at the right time with the right person.

I held her hands tightly. All theoretical knowledge doesn't work when love happens. So I preferred just to go with the flow.

She closed her eyes. Her breath took a pace the moment I touched her. All human bodies can't have the same temperature and that's why we feel a special pleasure when two bodies touch. She was quiet and softly I pushed her face to me. I touched her lips with my thumb and her lips started quivering. I came closer and could feel her warmth and gusts of her breaths on my lips. I couldn't control my feelings anymore.

Her warm breaths, and her fragrance overruled my senses. I kissed on her forehead and she lifted her head up and allowed me to move to her lips. Before going to her lips, I kissed on her eyes and then cheeks. She held my hand tightly and locked my lips with hers.

I would never express what I felt but the deeper she kissed me, the deeper I fell in love with her. We didn't open our eyes and kissed as long as we could and then we got a pace and that continued. I rubbed her lip-gloss with my tongue and finally she said, 'I love you.'

The moment she spoke, I didn't answer and without taking breath gave her a passionate deep kiss. We both felt like vacuum for a moment, 'I love you too. I just want to be with you for the rest of my life.'

She opened her eyes, looked at me with full of love, 'Will you always be with me?'

'You are not alone now. I am always with you,' I promised her, holding her hands tightly in mine.

Few tear drops came from my eyes and those were the drops of happiness.

'What happened?' she asked.

'Nothing, just…' I smiled.

'Mad you are, I am always with you.' She came close and kissed on those tear drops. Her lips were wet now and we had a long kiss that just went on for too long.

```
Yun toh nasha hum unki aaknon se karte hain,
haathon me pyala toh bas bahana tha.
```

First Valentine's Day with High Cut Briefs

In the month of winter, a cup of coffee and four hands, cold breeze early in the morning and few promises to be with each other. Yes, the day had come that symbolized love. Not very big but very small acts of love that made our love special.

The day came, Valentine's Day of the year 2010. The day to renew marriage vows for married couples and the day to make their feelings stronger for lovebirds who were dreaming of a life together. It's not about how many precious gifts and roses you get. It is all about how you spread love all around. Love can't be celebrated in a day. It has to be felt, trusted and promised forever.

Just a month before, she had set seven rules for our love in a diary while we were in the theatre, and I called it CUSTOMIZED RULES OF LOVE: RT3LSP, and those were:

1. Respect each other as individuals.
2. Time and dedication for each other.
3. Trust is a must.
4. There is no place for sacrifices but share grief with each other (Don't try to be smart…it's better we cry together. I have good cotton handkerchiefs to wipe tears.)

5. Lie but don't hurt (As you always lie to give me surprises but every time I catch you.)
6. Shout but never leave the other person alone (I have a right to shout but you can't leave me alone in any case.)
7. Passion in love.

Then we kissed each other passionately for very long until she bit my lower lip and wished me a very happy Valentine's Day over the call.

Things shall change, months shall pass but feelings and the spark of love will never die; such was my love for her. I was thinking about all those moments that I spent with her.

This was our first Valentine's Day. This had to be special and memorable. The best idea I had was not to gift any non-living things but to be present in front of her. Relationships don't demand gifts, those are just symbolic representation, they need faith, trust and dedication.

It's one of the difficult tasks to ask a girl for her size though I just had to ask her shoulder size. I called her.

'Hey do you have any T-shirt.'

'Don't be naughty at this moment,' she laughed. It was important for me to know the size, how to ask that was a question.

'Don't I have rights to know your size,' I tried a different card.

'Shut up. I am not going to tell you.'

'I love you,' I whispered. She didn't speak. I continued, 'I love you. May I hug you?'

'Yeah come.'

'Come to your bed,' I said.

'I am in my bed. Hug me. I missed you. Will you come to meet me?' We were lost in love and didn't ask anything anymore.

'I am hugging you and I miss you too. What are you wearing?'

'T-shirt and shorts.'

'May I kiss on your stomach?'

'Yeah kiss me.'

'Then push your t-shirt up.'

'Hmm…'

'I love you…,' I whispered again and felt her in my arms.

'I love you too. Hug me tightly,' she replied.

'I am hugging you and kissing on your stomach. Are you wearing innerwear?'

She didn't say a word and started kissing me. And this was the moment to know all her sizes and consider only one which I needed most that time – her shoulder size to order a t-shirt for her.

'Are you there,' she asked.

'Yes, I am here only. I will call you in sometime.' I disconnected the call. I was sure; she thought that I went to masturbate. Sometimes you have to lie but your lies shouldn't hurt anyone, it can be used to make people happy, smile or give surprises.

I ordered two customized t-shirts online, one with her funny photograph with showing finger and written below on the photograph- *Excuse me! What are you looking here?* And other with my photograph with blinking eyes saying that- *Look at me baby.* There was an intention behind to get these because I had planned for us to wear those t-shirts and roam around in streets of Delhi.

The day had come and I was there to meet her, to give her surprises and to re-live the moments.

'Good morning my love,' and I started speaking what actually I wanted to say-

```
This heart touched your heart on Valentine's
Day.
These lips touched your lips on Valentine's Day.
We kissed each other; we hugged each other,
```

```
No matter where we were…we just melted into each
other.
Your voice made me happy and I heard a loving
sound,
There was a special fragrance when you were
around.
You made the sky so blue,
And every moment was full of glee.
I feel like heaven when I think about you.
My heart stopped breathing when I couldn't find
you.
I water the rose of our love and it dries,
You look like a princess when I look into your
eyes.
My eyes are wet but feelings alive,
I will love only you, till the day I die.
```

'I just love the way you are, I am in love with you with every breath I take,' she said these lines with so much love and these days I lived for these moments only.

'I love you too. Wish you very happy Valentine's Day. I am standing at your college gate, I hope you won't be late,' I just said this at last.

'Are are you kidding me?' she was shocked as she didn't expect my arrival.

'Can't I be the best lover ever?'

'You are my best man ever. By the way today is Sunday so there is no college but just give me few minutes, I'll be there.'

'I didn't know any place except this, and take your time to dress up. I want you hard.'

'Shut up, let me get ready, bye.'

'Bye.'

'Listen,' she said.

'Yes,' I asked.

'I love you and you can kiss me hard today, bye…' She disconnected.

I was wearing that t-shirt. It was funny but this Valentine's Day didn't require any emotional moments, so it had to be funny.

She appeared. Oval face, black eyes, curved, well-shaped eyebrows like a bow, giving perfect contrast to her complexion. Chocolate color lip-gloss on her pink lips, her lips were like pulp of a flower. Her untied hair fell on her cheeks with a gust of wind. She was wearing blue-chocolate colored sweater, earphones in her ears, fish shaped earrings that hypnotized me for a moment, red cheeks, a cute face. She was looking just like I saw her a few weeks ago, even more beautiful.

'So finally you did this. And what's this?' she started laughing, pointing to my photograph on the t-shirt which I was wearing and the comment below- *Look at me baby.*

'I have one for you too,' I gave her the box.

'Oh really, then you are not allowed to be mad alone. Let me try that,' she excitedly took the box.

'You want to try here?'

'Shut up, this is my college, let's go inside, one gate is open there for library and many of the girls change after coming to college only.' I started at her.

'Don't look at me like this, I haven't done that but today I want to do that.'

We crossed all the ways and reached the washroom.

'Stay here, I will just come in a minute.'

How many minutes I spent standing in front of the ladies' washroom, I don't know. Few guys looked at me with f@#king weird faces. I just ignored them because there was no other option.

The moment she came out and I looked at the comment- *Excuse me! What are you looking here?* She repeated the words, 'Excuse me! What are you looking here,' and we both started laughing.

Have you ever liked coffee without sugar? Have you ever liked night without romance? We always like spicy food, coffee with light sugar and of course romantic nights. We didn't want to be like other couples so we just lived the way we were. 'Let's go to Rajouri Garden,' she said.

'Okay, let's go,' being lively and joyous, I winked at her.

We reached the mall in Rajori and while entering the mall she said, 'Now I want strawberry and chocolate ice-cream.' People were looking and smiling at us but who cared for others when we only lived for each other.

'Two?' I looked at her from top to bottom and grinned.

'Shut up, I am only 48kg,' she said very proudly.

'Then let's have three,' I laughed. We enjoyed ice cream with extra love.

'Come we'll buy something for you.' She pulled me to the escalators.

'For me?'

'Yes for you.' Usually she got excited when she bought something for her self but this time it was for me. After buying three-four t-shirts, she picked one more and said, 'Why don't you try this one?

It was funny, *three monkeys on t-shirt, first closing his eyes, second closing his ears, third closing his mouth and the fourth, a man putting hands on his zip with a comment 'Use condoms.'*

'So I should wear this t-shirt?' I looked at her sternly.

'When we wear this and roam around in mall then you can try this,' she blinked her eyes.

'Yes I can buy, if you buy that dress,' I pointed at the mannequin, a girl in half cup bra and high cut briefs, I laughed.

'Well I don't prefer your high cut briefs and cup size okay, I prefer thong, even you don't know that,' she gave me the sexiest smile ever.

'Okay my lord, my mistake. I am all in your service my lady.'

'Done? Now let's go.' We both laughed. She looked at me, 'What happened?'

'What if I wear your t-shirt and you wear mine?' we both looked at each other surprisingly.

'Are you sure?'

'Yes, I am.'

'What if we change together?' she teased me. I didn't speak and we headed towards the changing room.

We looked around and nobody was there, we didn't take much time to think and entered and locked the door. The moment the door was locked she hugged me tightly and kissed. To change we removed our t-shirts but didn't wear them for some time. We closed our eyes, hugged and just loved each other madly.

'I fulfilled my promise,' she grinned.

'Which promise?'

'To kiss me hardly, now let's go.'

She dressed me her t-shirt and I dressed her in mine.

'Happy Valentine's Day…,' We wished each other with a soft kiss and left.

Kabhi na sataya, kabhi na rulaya;
Teri chahathon me maine khud ko bhulaya
Tere he sang maine wo sapne dekhe;
Tere he sath ne mujhe jena sikhaya

I had to leave in the evening for college because day after tomorrow I had exams and I didn't want to be a dumb lover. I left in the evening and my mission was accomplished.

Things never really happen the way your expect them to be. Sometimes it turns out to be something far better and sometimes, well...

Why?

It always hurts when you hear this and especially when you are in relationship with that person. *Your call is on wait, please stay on the line or call again later.* It doesn't really mean that you are insecure but that's the human nature we all have.

This was happening from few weeks. Being irritated I asked, 'To whom you were talking, at least you could pick my call once.'

'I was talking to mom,' she replied arrogantly and indignantly she said, 'I'm not in a mood to talk, I can't talk to you.'

'I have been calling you from last forty minutes; at least you could pick my call. You could tell me once.'

'The way you doubt me, it's gory Anuj.'

'I don't doubt Pakhi, but every time it happens. I feel bad. We have college, friends and other stuff to do but I just said if you could pick my call and could tell me. Okay I won't say anything, anymore. Did you have your dinner?'

'No, I am hungry, just going for dinner. I'll talk to you later,' she disconnected without saying love you. This never happened before. I was amiable but she behaved very impertinently. I pampered but she showed her dissonance.

Things were not going fine but I always believed that it won't affect the way we loved each other. Distance relationships are tough to maintain but we had been managing so well.

It was May 29. 11:58 pm, I called to wish her birthday. She didn't pick the call, might be she was sleeping so I called her again. *Your call is on wait, please stay on the line or call again later.* I wanted to be the first guy to wish her and I couldn't. Moreover, it made me very uncomfortable to know that she was talking to someone else.

When she picked my call, I sang a song for her and somehow I asked who called her first. She felt joyous and told me that it was her college friend Arpan.

'A guy?' I thought for a moment and ignored. We talked for few minutes then she said, 'Talk to you later, everybody is calling me.'

'Wish you very happy birthday, enjoy your day,' I kissed and wished her. Early morning I called her up and spoke what I was writing from last night.

```
If you'll look at me, I'll come to you;
If you'll hug me, I'll never leave you,
Did you miss me? I'll never ask you;
I will be always behind you.
When I look at you, I feel sweetness in my
heart,
When I think about you, I can feel your presence
around me.
Your presence made me happy, your presence made
me cry
But I love the way you are, I don't know why.
```

'I'm sorry I shouted at you last night, love you,' she pampered and asked for a hug.

'It's okay, I love you too. Just few days remaining then I am coming to Delhi for next two months, everything will be fine.' Love was in the air and I was flying with my angel. We both became a need for each other. Excess of everything is bad; we proved it wrong as we were on call almost all the time.

It was August 2010, days were normal but nights were pleasant and sweet and why not, I was with my soul mate. I looked at the sky and I could feel their love for the sky when a group of birds flew so high and the sky just released them freely. I could just feel it. Even birds were playing with me. When I tried to look at them, they hid themselves in clouds and when I turned my eyes to the other side, again they came out of clouds. It was like they were celebrating their happiness with me for a special day. They were enjoying in the sky and we were dreaming under the moon light every night and making them true in the morning.

'Get up, I want to talk,' she said over the call with her lovely voice.

'It's morning, give me a hug and sleep,' I rolled in bed and hugged my pillow imagining her in my arms.

'But we have lots more things to do like we can video chat on Gmail,' she said, without leaving any option to say 'No' and I never wanted to say 'No' for any of her wishes.

'Early morning...' I asked her in sleep.

'Just get up and check. I'm not able to install the webcam, it's not working,' she continued till the time I got up and logged in my laptop.

'I'll do, don't worry, give me your password,' I asked.

'You're online, I will ping you on G-talk,' she disconnected the call. A message window popped up on right side of the screen.

Pakhi: Abha221188 is the password.

Me: Okay, give me a minute, I will just check. By the way, nice password, aunty's name and my date of birth.

If you have senses to make decision, to understand between good and bad, you are considered as human. There are other natures also which define your existence like, thinking about someone, loving someone and being possessive. I know you are a true Indian lover, you do the same thing. Before installing web-cam, intentionally I clicked on sent items, just to see which songs and photograph she sent me last time. I started smiling looking at them; photographs, songs, poems, love letters and few porn clips, which were sent to my mail id anujtiwari.official@gmail.com

A pop up message flashed again on the screen.

Pakhi: Done?
Me: Wait…

I moved cursor to few more mails and remembered all those naughty moments we shared. I found her voice mails that I saved in my laptop to listen whenever I'd miss her or feel alone. I couldn't find any other voice-mails but I found one mail saying-

Dear,

I am thinking about you. We are so close here and it's not like I'm feeling you are far. It's just that I want to let you know again how much I'm in love with you. I'll love you forever and for always, baby. You are all mine. I don't know what good I did in this life to deserve you but it must have been very good and I ended up with you!

Being with you makes me feel like the entire world is mine. I love you, baby, and I'm yours forever!

Only yours

This cut the nerves because it wasn't sent to me. Things just got worst in my mind. All negative things connected the dots and made a hoodwink. On May 25th, just five days before, she sent that mail to ajay16…@gmail.com.

Once she told me about Ajay, that they were together when she prepared for CPMT in Delhi and then we never discussed about it because once in a while it happens in life with everyone. Every person has a past and if we pay too much attention to those memories, they hurt back. However after looking at that mail, a cold chill ran through the calves of my legs. I never expected that from her. I lost my senses and anger on my face. All promises seemed like in vain. I felt darkness in front of my eyes for a moment.

'We are talking from last 11 months and why did it happen? Why didn't she tell me, is something going wrong? I felt helpless and why she didn't discuss this with me when she had discussed everything. I didn't know in which situations that mail was sent but that broke my trust.

A pop up message again appeared on the screen.

Pakhi: You there?

Me: I will just come.

'Wrong is wrong, doesn't matter in which situation you have done,' I thought, heap of questions flooded in my mind, and all were unanswered. I remembered everything, whatever happened on May 25th. We fought that day, when I asked her to whom she was talking. She had replied giving excuse of her mother. I started getting the answers. She was continuously messaging me on g-talk.

Pakhi: What are you doing? I am waiting.

Me: Wait, I will just call you.

I remembered all those moments that we spent together. When we kissed for the first time, when she put her hands on my chest, when we shared chocolate, enjoyed flavour of cold drink through mouth, when she put her teeth on my neck to give me love bite, and when we just kissed each other deep to our soul.

'Were those moments unreal?'

I closed the lid of laptop.

'I love you a lot. Why have you done this with me, why...?' I started fighting with my thoughts inside which gave me nothing else. Cell phone flashed with a message-

```
What happened, why are you not replying on
g-talk?'
```

I had mixed feelings that time and I knew if I would pick her call something would surely happen which would not be favourable for us. I left a message-

```
I will just come in few minutes. Need to go
urgently.
```

Things shouldn't be pulled out of the coffin when buried. Many things happen in our life which give us few good and few bad things along. Things which give us a lesson to learn should be made the past and which give us reason to smile should always be in nature. I had to ask about that mail she sent to Ajay but there is always a right time and I was waiting for that. Before I could lose myself in knotted thoughts which tried to grip me, my cell phone beeped with one more message-

```
Do you love me? I am missing you. Can we talk?
```

Whenever she said these words, I was there for her and never wanted to break this faith that she had built up with me. I called her and we talked happily with no confusion, no excuses and lots of love that we always did.

Web cam was installed but there were many things behind the camera but I didn't care about those and just loved her. We used to start our day with web-cam and end with late night phone calls. Though we were far away but we both explored each other's soul. Now nothing was hidden except few questions which I had decided to ask at the right time.

Those three words always made me crazy about her. I remembered the days we spent together. Those sweet and sour moments made us happy. Her voice made me feel like; few roses touched my cheeks and whispered in my ears, 'I love you'.

```
I love the way you are...I love the way you are.
Every day, I love you more than yesterday.
```

How long we started our journey?
How long we made milestone together?
How many promises we made together?
And I hoped, she'd never break my heart...

Aunties of Indian Families

There are certain things which make us different from others. I always wanted to do something different in my life and whenever I looked for that my mom slapped on my face and I was back to my studies. When I started understanding the things around I came to know about the reason of being engineer. If your neighbour is a doctor or an engineer, anyhow you have to be. Luckily or unluckily I had both, so one thing was sure that either I'd be an engineer or a doctor. This is not the end; you have to get ready for their questions and suggestions-

```
1. How's placement in your college?
2. When will you get a good job?
3. How much you scored in last exam?
4. You are an engineer, please repair my
   computer/fan-regulator, etc.
5. Side by side look for government job as
   well.
6. Is food not good at college or is there
   any matter of girl?
```

Though last question was correct but my answers were also in the same way every time, 'No aunty, engineering is so tough, we don't even get time to think about anything else and if someday I find someone, of course will tell you first. Genuine answers for genuine questions.

Free suggestions are always available so I treated them in that way only; just ignored and did what I wanted to do. I was watching movie on my laptop when my cousin Kavya entered the room. Many sand castles we made together, so shared a good bonding. I paused when we had fun. She took my laptop and clicked on folder win32.

'Who's she?' she asked, her eyes slightly squinting, as if she didn't like her.

'Just a friend,' tried to ignore her.

'Are you sure? I know just a friend,' she smiled, she liked her but was confused why her photograph was in my laptop.

I asked the same question myself, 'What is she doing in my laptop, she should be here in front of me…forever…my soulmate.'

'What's going on here, he doesn't have anything to do and you are also into,' mom looked at us; we laughed, and then looked at each other.

Mom came to me and asked, 'When are you leaving for Noida?'

I knew that she wasn't happy with my departure because she wanted me to be at home and to spend time with family.

'Mom, just after a week,' I tried to make her happy, pulled her hands and stood up.

'When will you come back?' she asked.

'Just after my summer training, I'll come back.'

'Can't you enjoy your summer vacations with us and join any of the institutes which suit you. You can discuss with your dad to join BSNL if you feel so.'

'Yes, mom but nothing suits me here and I don't want to join BSNL. People are lazy over there,' I contradicted.

'Your dad is working there from the day you were born, even before that. Your sister has done masters in computers, you're doing engineering, we have a nice place to live happily, still do you really think people these are lazy.'

'Mom I didn't mean that. He is my hero but I want to learn something,' I replied despondently. My mind gave a strong punch... Oh learning!

```
When you are in love, you do things for your
love and compromise with many other things.
```

We both had fixed our summer schools in Delhi so that we could spend time with each other. We both were from different skills, different places but destination was same...to be with each other... to love each other. Chronically we were drawing a picture of a new journey...JOURNEY OF TWO HEARTS.

'I'll fill colors in that picture when she'll come to my home forever,' I said to myself, closed my eyes and felt mellow music, her beauty, my beauty and everything seemed completed.

```
When you are in love, you never look back,
you ignore everything but just live for that
person, and I was at the same phase.
```

So, I reached the hostel of Jaypee Institute of Engineering, Noida on the morning of May 24th. I was tired, sweating in the sunny day. I unlocked the room, switched on air ducts, relaxed for few minutes. I leaned back in the chair and put one leg over the arm of the chair, I was missing home.

I explored the room, opened the windows and looked out and then again closed them. Walls were painted as I could smell, table was full of dust, and I closed my eyes for few minutes.

After ignoring few calls and service messages on the screen, I called Pakhi.

'Hey...what's up?' I asked placing my bag into the cupboard.

'Nothing, where are you?' she asked me very eagerly.

'I just reached few minutes before,' I replied with tiredness.

When there is no naughtiness, there is no flavour of love. I added, 'Ok, see you tomorrow, I'm very tired.'

'Hm…ok,' she replied, no words after that.

'Ok, bye,' I disconnected.

At the next moment, phone flashed, a message- What happened? Did I do anything wrong?

I didn't reply, and left for bath, dressed well and then called her again.

'Miss gorgeous, get ready I'll reach Anand Vihar in next thirty minutes,' I replied boisterously.

'I knew it! How come Mr. Tiwari told me to meet tomorrow. By the way why did you not tell me that time, now I have to get ready,' she asked blandly.

'Because I love you so much, now get ready and come soon,' I kissed.

'Okay, bye. See you.'

And then we Met Again

'Should I close my eyes,' I thought looking at those pretty girls in mini skirts and sleeveless tops. I was standing at the Anan Vihar Metro Station near the ticket counter. I didn't cross the checkpoint and was waiting for her.

'You are committed,' My mind told me very sternly. I looked at one of them who was talking to her boyfriend over phone. Her other phone rang and that gave me a reason to start dissecting the situation. She looked at her other phone, which was still ringing in her left hand. Her boyfriend emerged from the other side of the escalator and started approaching her. She looked at him and smiled, turned her face a bit to hide her phone from her neck and whispered. I could understand what she said, 'I'll call you in the evening, don't call me, I am with family. I'll be busy, love you too.' I had studied few concepts in mathematics-One to Many and Many to One but implementation I saw there and a confusion got cleared about how sex ratio is maintained in our country.

After a few minutes, I could see her on the escalator. She seemed over a call and all the scenes of a few minutes before re-played in my mind.

In white *kurti* and blue *salwar*, she looked gorgeous. Few drops of sweat on her forehead claimed how much she loved me and few drops of water that just dropped from corners of her lips when she removed water-bottle from her mouth claimed how did she manage herself. She

103

took out a handkerchief and wiped her face which looked red. I smiled at her and she disconnected saying, 'Bye ma.'

We see many things happening around us; those might be considered as good or bad according to us. However the reality says, there is nothing called good and bad, or white and black, it's actually gray always. It depends upon us ,how we look at it. Something which is harmful for us might be helpful for someone else. Killing a deer is a crime but if a tiger kills, it's his hungriness. So we shouldn't make any perception just because of others. Whatever comes from out heart always gives the right decision, that's why we are told to listen to our soul's advice. My heart had accepted her as my soul mate, so there was nothing that could take my attention in any other directions.

'Do you have *kajal*,' I asked, taking water bottle from her hand.

'Why?' she asked surprisingly as without any greeting, I just asked this weird question.

'I have to put some just below your ears to save you from evil eye.'

'Crazy guy you are, come, let's go,' she laughed and pulled my hand. Whenever I saw her cheeks, I always remembered ad of ponds cold cream – googly woogly woosh. Her half-covered forehead with hair when she set her hair with first three fingers just above the left ear, she looked stunning. Her dangle earrings were trying to touch her neck and looked as if they were trying to kiss her neck repeatedly. I could inhale her fragrance that connected to the moment when I kissed her for the first time in a movie theatre. My wishes got intense to hug her and never let her go.

Without asking each other, we both knew where we had to head for. There was no better idea than watching movie together in an empty theatre where we could spend a good time together. We were getting down at Noida sector-18 metro station, a small girl and a boy came in front of us with a red rose, with an expectation that I'd buy for Pakhi. I ignored and moved ahead.

'Hey wait,' she said.

'This silent Sardar is not doing anything for them, at least I can do something,' pointing out to congress hording just above poor children, she took her lunch box and gave it to them. I was surprised but happy, actually got mixed feelings for a moment.

'Do you think, doing this would give them a bright future,' I generally asked her.

'I know, I can't change the country but I can change myself. Now let's go else we will end our day with rubbish political discussions.'

The charm that she carried made me smile inside and we headed to TGIP mall.

```
Only LEFT and RIGHT hand can hold each other and
walk together...
Only RIGHTs are enough to say bye. Nobody is
perfect in the world, if you Love the perfection
of his/her imperfections then LOVE exists.
```

'Two tickets, Robin Hood, 12:30 show, wall corner,' I said very blandly, looking at the ticket counter girl and this time I wasn't hesitated to ask for corner seats. There is always a right time for right things like, to ask for corner seats or to ask for condom or to ask for pads. Though I was at the first stage but time comes with the right opportunity and happily I grabbed that.

'Sir, fifth row from the back, two tickets, 12:30 show,' lady from the counter said.

I nodded, paid and we moved.

'It seems only you and I have come to watch the movie,' slackly she said.

'Do you want me to call other girls to sit with me,' I teased her, looked around us, and shrugged my shoulder. We were seated on K-1, K-2.'

Few things never change, love of a mother and ad of Vicco turmeric- *vicco turmeric nahi cosmetic vicco turmeric ayurvedic cream.*

Till the time it was playing, she held my hand and said, 'Don't you think so you should change your watch?'

'Yeah, there are scratches; I'd change it next time.'

'Why next time, change it now,' she grinned, opened her bag, rummaged around in her purse and slowly she took a small packet out of it.

'Is this for me?' boisterously and spiritedly I asked. She un-wrapped the box and tied that watch on my hand.

'Hey, it's nice. Thank you so much,' I caressed her cheeks. She took a deep breath and felt relaxed with my gentle touch on her cheeks. She responded very slowly and very attractively, took all my attention into her eyes. I placed my right hand on her left.

'Don't you believe in giving return gifts?' she whispered around ears and played with my fingers.

'Do you really want me to give you return gift.'

'Don't you want to stretch these moments and now you have a watch too,' she grinned.

'I love you baby,' I poured more love in my eyes.

This time I just held her hand tightly on my chest. I placed my other hand on the back of her neck. She looked at me but didn't say even a single word. Her half-opened eyes looking at the screen, my four fingers on her neck; and thumb just below her ears. I rubbed her cheeks three four times with my thumb. She closed her eyes and shrank. I removed my hand from her neck and set her hair, came close to her ear, 'I love you baby, you are looking pretty,' I whispered.

She shivered and I kissed on her cheeks. I looked at her opened lips. I came close to her. She placed her hand on my lap and other on my neck. I could feel her passion, when she ran her hand from my neck to stomach. I looked at her and fervidly I kissed on her lips. She wasn't in senses now, her eyes were closed. I could feel her warmth from her mouth. I rubbed my tongue on her soft pink lips; thinking that a kiss is important to be healthy. Desire ignited the world around us as we became lost in a sea of lust and love. The rest of the world was engulfed in our lustful burning flames as our kisses grew more urgent. As our lips pulled apart, a gentle breeze fluttered over the flames of desperate heat. Our breathing came out in short, desperate gasps. It was gentle, but captivating, a mixture of sweet root-beer and salty ocean water. Mesmerized lips pressed together time after time, transporting us to another world.

Her saliva met mine, rubbed her front teeth with my tongue. Ragged breathing and dancing tongues brought a fiery heat to the cold ocean air. With just the two of us there, the rest of the world disappeared for a moment. It was a spicy, powerful combination that sent waves of passion crashing over us. The intensity had washed away. The rest of the world was slowly coming back into focus. Our lips were claiming our tongues to win the game of lust in which we were lost and then suddenly…

Girlfriend or No Girlfriend - Come to Delhi

Someone said – sit properly. We both were stunned and released our hands wherever they were. It was the security person who roamed around and a took a complete round of the theatre in between the movie. It was a little embarrassing because it was happening on other seats as well but we were caught at the very wrong moment. I didn't understand why they poked their ass when we had paid the ticket charges including all entertainment taxes. I kept holding her hands till the movie got over and so did the taste of her strawberry lip gloss from my mouth.

Delhi is one of the most happening cities. I wished to spend more time. I was as I got to roam around with the one with whom I was going to spend the rest of my life. I didn't know where to go, I only knew how to love and romance. She had an idea and I executed that very well with surprises.

'I'll show you Delhi today,' exiting the theatre she said.

'I am always at your service to follow your judgments, my lord,' I locked fingers in her and smiled.

'Rare creature,' she laughed and we headed to board the metro to CP.

Delhi is always about hang out zones and famous joints which are popular amongst all, and give a taste of this city as well. We had already planned the places to visit and were excited to explore the well-known Delhi hang out zones like Connaught Circle. The huge beautiful structured houses and the biggest market place in Delhi where you can be sure of finding anything and everything. *Janpath,* the market area with a string of small shops displaying Indian products, Indian traditional clothes; along the way there were also women selling beaded wall hangings, ivory earrings, wooden masks and alluring necklaces and similar items, and a lovely circular bookshop and flower stall.

Paranthe wali gali which is a famous lane in the Chandni Chowk area of Delhi that has been serving *paranthas* of different varieties since the 1870's. City Walk, Rajori, Kamla Market and many other places to have a bite of Delhi Street delicacies. Even we had fun and frolic attitude of Delhi people and going around in the city gave a completely new experience.

How could I forget to roam around Delhi University's North Campus. The happening place is always buzzing with smart college crowd and beautiful Delhi girls. We visited BYD- Big Yellow Door which was the best spot for college crowd and most student friendly place. We just loved BOMB burger of BYD which made our tummy full and we enjoyed the day to the fullest. World seemed so small, happiness connected each thread of love between us; life seemed so beautiful and colourful.

After few days, she started going to Rao IAS classes as she had the most versatile mind that changed within seconds. She had to do MSc and then MBA, then jewellery designing and she ended up with IAS preparation. At some point of time, she spoke the same words as my mom used to say to me to join IAS classes but I said, 'Engineering is enough to give me pain, I won't be able to sustain more.'

We used to meet at Yamuna Bank metro station after my training classes and I dropped her at her IAS classes in the evening. It was memorable time for me when I kept waiting outside at the bus stop while her classes went on for two hours from four to six in the evening. It looked stupid but I used to wait for her and that made me smile, laugh, and sometimes weird when few people asked if I needed any help or why I was standing there for so long.

And then after her classes we used to go to *Janpath* and roamed around in CP till night. The other day it started raining and she had to have *gola*. We can never forget that day.

'I need one *gola*,' she pulled me and approached towards *gola wala*.

'You're not well.'

'Just one, please.'

'It's raining, you're not well and you are having *gola*,' I said her, looking at her and then the gola guy.

'Just one minute, *bhaiya ek kala katta and ek mix wala*,' Pakhi bought.

'Come it's 9:00 pm, you are getting late, and it's raining,' I pulled her left hand. We took auto rickshaw from CP to Anand Vihar. It was pleasant and romantic and we didn't care about time or about how many signals we had to cross.

Walking hand in hand, the rain, the cold breeze, and the kala khatta with the gori girl.

'Thanks.'

'For what?' I asked.

'For the best day ever,' she said, holding my hands.

I pointed her towards the front mirror through which usually the rickshaw guy would look at others. She smiled, held hands more tightly.

'Tomorrow we'll go to *Chandni Chowk*.'

'Tomorrow, you have to go to your classes,' I said, touched her cheeks and pinched softly.

'Then I'll bunk my classes,' she pinched back on my cheeks.

'No need to bunk classes, we'll go later.'

Pakhi replied and assured me, 'Tomorrow's class isn't important, so we can go to *Chandni Chowk*, I have to buy few books too.'

'*Aapke aage main natmastak hu prabhu,*' I laughed.

'Ok we'll go.'

'You are so sweet.'

'Yes, I am.'

We came out from auto-rickshaw.

Coffee, ice-cream, *kala khatta* in rains, no limits, no boundaries, just love, wet evening, hands in hands, crazy go lucky, we made the day we wanted to live.

Next day we both missed our classes. One side where my friends were in training institute, another side we were having *Kachori* in *Chandni Chowk*. We both loved that place *parathe wali gali*.

Her hands were in her pocket and I was feeding her piece by piece. In between, I put a piece of chilly and was ready to see her dance.

'Shhh...Shhhh...Shhh....Mirchi...pani...' Pakhi asked for water.

'Hahaha....Nooo,' I laughed.

'I'll kill you Anuj, give me water,' Pakhi jumped at the same place multiple times.

'First say you love me,' I choked her.

'I love you, so much...muaahh...muaahh...muahh, give me water,' Pakhi asked for water. *Kachori wale bhaiya* looked at us, smiled, and gave a glass of water.

'Hahaha...sorry...I wanted to hear love you,' I said, touching my finger on her cheeks.

'Youuu...I'll kill you,' Pakhi pushed me back.

We moved ahead and then somewhere she found *lassi* shop.

'Hey Anuj,' Pakhi said.

'What?'

'Hey Anuj.'

'*Kya hua baccha?*' I asked.

'*Suno na, woo...,*' Pakhi pointed towards *lassi* shop.

'Hahaha...motu, come, crazy girl,' we both moved to that lassi shop.

'*Bhaiya ek lassi dena,*' I took a glass. One big glass of *lassi* and Pakhi took only few sips, 'Now I can't,' Pakhi said, wiping her mouth with her hands.

'Done...only two sips,' I wiped curd from her lips corner.

'Let's go.'

We just moved from there and then I saw a shop, written on the board '*Jaleba* Shop.'

'Look, you want to try?' I asked her.

'Yup let's go,' Pakhi looked at me, held my hand and laughed, 'Why not, don't leave any chance to feel regret in life.'

'How will you go home?'

'Shut up, I am not drunk.'

```
I love the way you are, I love the way you talk.
I love the way you look, I love the way you
hook.
I love the way you tease, I love the way to
breeze.
I love the way you shout, I love the way you
cry.
I don't know what you are but I love the way
you are.
```

Every day a new lesson, a new chapter and a new story of our love story unfolded. This journey became memorable for us, journey of love, JOURNEY OF TWO HEARTS.

I Secretly Want You

After spending a month together now it was time to pack the bags. We were sitting at Fio restaurant of The Garden of Five Senses. It was a beautiful garden and delivered energy with happiness. After seeing entire Delhi in a month, the variety of attractions left us spellbound and we did not feel like leaving the place at all. The garden covered a huge area. There was perfect silence and I just wanted to keep my head on her shoulder.

'Is it necessary to go?' she asked placing her hand on my head.

'Don't worry whenever I'll get holidays, I'll come again,' I replied and continued, 'Hey tomorrow we'll meet. But come early.' It was the last day in Delhi so I wanted to make it special in my ways.

'Tomorrow is Sunday, and it won't be possible to come early morning, *nanu-nani*, *mama ji* everybody will be at home and why don't you stay for few more days. This week we have a marriage ceremony at home and you can meet my family if you wish so,' she smiled and of course she wanted me to stay and to meet her family.

Meeting a girl's entire family is the second toughest thing after impressing the girl's brother and father.

'I'm not invited and I don't know anyone,' I wanted to meet her family because it might be the first step to reach the destination.

'I am inviting you now and *ma* knows about you,' she grinned and looked confident that I'd stay for few more days for her.

'Tomorrow let's meet and let's do something.' We both left and I remembered all legendary lovers Romeo-Juliet, Heer-Ranjha, Robin Hood-Maid Marian and then about us. It's not as easy as we think to fall in love and make it the best love story.

Next day we were supposed to meet in afternoon but I got ready early morning because I had to do so many things to make our last day memorable for us...forever. There are few things which are essential for any departure as I was not sure to stay to meet her family because I was invited with no prior plans. So I bought a chocolate cake, candles and a romantic novel and a surprise gift. Gifts are not to show how rich you are, those are to make you remember the moments you spent with that person and we already had a series of memories. I boarded the metro from Noida sec-18 and reached EDM mall. When I entered the mall, I saw someone entering the Archie's gallery who looked just like her from the back but as she hadn't reached so I ignored and considered that it happens when you are in love.

'Where are you?' I asked her over a call.

'Just reaching,' she responded. Taking the escalators I reached on the top floor in the food-court area. I put the cake and gifts on the table. I was excited but somewhere I was unhappy with departure. Someone came from the back and said- Hello. Yes, I was tracked and caught. The one I saw entering Archie's was Pakhi indeed.

'You are already here,' I looked at her.

'I saw you, when you entered the mall, I caught you and I would at every moment Mr. Tiwari,' being so happy and lively she said.

'I am always ready to be hijacked, Miss. Gorgeous.' We laughed.

```
LOVE is like a healthy competition, if someone
loves you, you always try to love more and
in counter that person proves you wrong. That
makes it lively, cheerful and long lasting. Now
```

```
you can't just sit at home with lighted candles
waiting for your partner. You need to go out,
do some hard work and be as active as you're in
bed. No-one needs to follow other to make their
love story best, Just make your own.
```

'But this is not fair. Now go and come after two minutes. I did hard work to make it possible, so I won't let it go like this.'

'Ok, Ok, I will go, you crazy creature.'

She went and I put a candle in centre of the cake, managed everything properly as per the plan and then called her.

'So sweet of you,' she looked at me and I could remember all the memories. Sometimes happiness is to do something for someone you love.

'I don't know what's the occasion but you can consider this my farewell,' I put my head down in Chinese tradition to welcome.

She became emotional and her eyes were full with tears of love, and I was not going to wipe her tears because these tears were of love, life, family, friendship, memories and all the stupid things we did. I promised myself, someday I'd surely write our 'Journey of Two Hearts' because 'It Had to Be You.'

'Now cut it,' I said as the candle dropped a few drops of wax around. We cut the cake, laughed, enjoyed, and lived few last moments before my departure. Celebration was not over; she took out a box from her bag and gifted me.

'What's that?' I asked.

'Open it.'

'Okay,' I smiled.

'Hey slowly,' she said sitting on the stool.

'I can't. Wow, nice, alarm watch. I actually needed it. Now you have all the right to wake me up without any excuses,' I looked at her and grinned. She poured love in her eyes, touched my hands, 'Don't go,' said she.

'I'll come soon?' I patted her and pinched her nose. I took a box out of my bag.

'What's in it?' excitedly she asked.

'You can open it,' I just smiled. She opened the box in seconds. Girls are actually as fast in unwraping gifts as boys are in taking off their inner wears.

'Oh my god,' she was just shocked. It was a beautiful dress. She continued with her expressions, 'But that day you said, it was not good.'

'Because I wanted to get this for you and I'd like it.'

'You are actually a mad guy. Can't believe but salute my lord, your choice is just awesome. This is my best dress now,' she looked happy and I wanted to make her so.

'Well, I have something more for you,' she wiped her tears and gave me a pocket card. That card said- It just takes the will to succeed; all you have to do is say 'I will.'

'Now let me write something more for you,' she took the gift wrapper and wrote- 'Time may be good or bad, I'm always with you.' I kept those cards in my wallet to be there forever; they still make me smile when I look at them.

We missed each other inside but we decided not to say good bye because we both knew anyone cried, the other would not be able to go away. We left. I got her message:

```
This is for you- I just have few words to say
that I'lll miss you a lot. The time we spent
together in last few weeks is unforgetable.
It'd difficult to be like this but we'll be on
call and chats, so we'll manage. You know, I
```

really loved the way you waited for me during my classes and the way you surprised me. I love you.

Moreover one important thing, I forgot to mention that girls have all the rights to get angry and this is the duty of boys that they should pamper them in spite of sitting alone. Got it Mr. Perfect?

I love you!!!

Typical Indian Marriage

I was again going through the message she sent, rolling in my bed. She insisted me to stay for few more days. You have to make few compromises in your life to achieve something. Giving a thought to this I stayed to meet her family and decided to attend- The typical Indian wedding.

I was excited to meet her family but nervous too as I had heard they ask weird questions just not to give their daughter's hand in yours. However, I was smart enough I planned to implement the training that I got as a child spending much time with aunties. Someone has said rightly. The things we learn in childhood days stay forever and I had thought enough on how to impress my future in-laws.

Just to make it spicier, I decided to reach at the venue directly as Pakhi already had given me the invitation card. I entered to attend her cousin's marriage ceremony. I had attended many ceremonies with my mother. Something was common in all the weddings and it'd continue forever.

Indian women wear their finest jewellery at weddings. I couldn't find any nude neck and any shortage of gold. Doesn't matter how much the gold price rises or goes down but that can't affect neck, hand, waist of our Indian women. It was the largest gold exposition. The things I observed were not at all funny. If you are a girl under 30, anyhow you'll be married by the end of the wedding events or you will definitely find a suitable match as per family discussions because finding you a partner will be the mission of every auntie who has met you just once or twice. These Indian weddings are actually about families and not the young couple, they are just this target of the occasion. I was just worried about the marriage couple as there were so many counters of delicious food and deserts which they couldn't have. People were prepared to loosen that drawstring on salwar and open those belt holes a bit and that couple could only stair at them, nothing else could be done.

It was actually a Punjabi wedding. Her cousin was getting married with Punjabi guy…Love marriage! I was happy to see both of them, as that meant that there was a scope for us too.

```
I never believed in that. CASTE DEFINES LOVE OR
LOVE DEFINES LOVE; Indian families are confused
these days, they look at the last name first
before looking at the person. (On one side they
talk about our ancient time and worship of
Brahma, Vishnu and Mahesh and on another side
they say, their religion doesn't allow us to
do this. Do they really know the last name of
Brahma, Vishnu and Mahesh?) But I was happy with
my bird of desires…PAKHI and hoped to merge both
the surnames together, though biologically we
were one already.
```

'It's not a dream, can you pinch me,' she saw and ran to me.

'How can I make you sad,' I just smiled. She set my collar and looked around being conscious.

'I love you,' she winked.

'I love you too. Where is everyone?' I whispered.

First impressions can be lasting impressions. That first meeting with the in-laws usually takes place long before anyone thinks seriously of walking down the aisle.

'Come and meet my family,' she pulled my hand and headed towards the *Havan Kund*. My heart beats started running fast and I was nervous.

'Anuj! Why are you looking lost? What happened?' she turned and we paused.

'Hey, stop. We shouldn't disturb them, they seem busy.' I pulled her hand. I rearranged my shirt, set my hair like a kid and took a deep breath. I smiled at her. Very important thing that I knew was, one should keep away from males at the in-laws' home, as they will try to pull your leg and ask weird questions. In Indian families, the toughest part is to make the father, elder brothers and other elders happy. Therefore, I prepared myself to smile at silly jokes and to agree to whatever crap they would say.

'Today only two people are busy, the one who is wearing the turban and the other who forced him to wear that; and Anuj, she's my mother, not your boss. No need for formalities,' she called her mother. I started memorizing our values, culture and tradition. I was gulping air and her mother came.

'Be cool and just chill,' she smiled, blushed and looked happy but I looked nervous. 'A-N-U-J-J-J...' she looked at me and held my hand when nobody was watching. That moment I observed everything about *Shadi-ka-pandal* from lighting to shoes except not to meet her parents so soon. The fragrances of roses and lavender filled the air.

'Mom, this is Anuj,' she said to her mother. Pakhi pointed her hand first to me and then to her mother in respect, 'Anuj, my mom...'

'How are you beta?' she asked.

I came forward and touched her feet, 'Namaste, aunty.' I nodded with a reply, 'Good.' *Chura* in her cousin's hand broke my sight that was stuck at *Havan Kund*. Pakhi grinned and blinked at me when I touched her mom's feet. The first card worked, I felt happy. Long way to go, I thought.

Her mother was wearing a red sari with a golden border with heavy work on that. The way she talked made me conscious for a moment. I wanted to call her Ma as she was going to be my mother-in-law but I stopped myself.

'No stupidity…no stupidity,' I remembered.

'So, did you have something?' aunty asked and broke my reverie.

'Yeah, I'll have, I'm good.' I smiled and responded very politely. I didn't talk to my own mother like this. Everything was fine and I was comfortable now. Mother-in-laws are not that bad. I felt so. They are bad only in Ekta Kapoor's serials.

After sometime, people started moving to buffet which was at the centre of the *pandaal*. Most of the people were separated because of the buffet. I felt awkward standing alone. Nevertheless, my eyes were looking at sweet girls and sexy women, the Indian beauty. What to wear and how to wear who knew better than Delhi beauties, front, side, back, everything was perfect. I always hated the curves in mathematics but I never missed the opportunity to feel them in my real life.

Nobody knew that we were in love, so we had to hide "us". We both sat near the *Kund* after having dinner.

'Hey, what are you thinking?' she asked, dragging herself to my side.

'Nothing,' I blinked my eyes, dreamt for our future for a while and asked, 'Where is uncle?'

'He wasn't well, so he came for some time and went back,' she replied. She looked sad as her father was the one who fulfilled her wishes with no questions.

'Should I also stay awake the whole night here?' I asked her to keep the conversation on a different track where she can be comfortable and happy. I didn't want to hurt her.

'Yes whole night. It's not easy to get a girl,' she held my hand and hiding it from people's sight. Sweetness of sweets in the weather, smell of spices, noise of gossips, shouting of old people somewhere, still I could feel wide awake, even well after the midnight.

'Now stop looking at her, she is getting married,' she laughed and gave punch on my ribs.

'Logically it's my right to tease her, she is my so called future *saali*,' I pinched her waist and an uncle saw us.

'Oucchhh...' she shouted. People around *havan kund* turned back, looked at us.

I murmured, 'What the F...'

'Ma cockroach...,' she pretended as she saw cockroach and I was un-blamed.

'Why did you pinch me, someone could have seen us,' she pushed me, again gave a strong punch. Someone came from the back, 'How are you Pakhi beta?' He tried to dye his hair but somehow he missed somewhere as I could see. I looked at his broad eyebrows and smiled, 'Namaste uncle.' He smiled but looked at me as I kissed her daughter with a devil's sight. He was her uncle who saw us when I pinched on her waist. I took my cell phone and started doing something just to ignore him and remembered- *one should keep away from males at the in-laws' home, as they will try to pull your leg and ask weird questions.*

It was 3:30am, when few were feeling sleepy, few were in sleep and only few were actually participating in the marriage ceremony with groom. Both victims stood up and *Pandit ji* started delivering seven vows of Hindu marriage:

1. The bride and the groom take the first step of the seven vows to pledge that they would provide a prospered living for the household or the family and that they would look after and avoid those who might hinder their healthy living.

2. During the second step of the seven *pheras*, the bride and the groom promise that they would develop their physical, mental and spiritual powers in order to lead a lifestyle that would be healthy.

3. During the third vow, the couple promises to earn a living and increase it by righteous and proper means, so that their materialistic wealth increases manifold.

4. While taking the fourth vow, the married couple pledges to acquire knowledge, happiness and harmony by mutual love, respect, understanding and faith.

5. The fifth vow is taken to expand their heredity by having children, for whom, they will be responsible. They also pray to be blessed with healthy, honest and brave children.

6. While taking the sixth step around the sacred fire, the bride and the groom pray for self-control of the mind, body and soul and longevity of their marital relationship.

7. When the bride and the groom take the seventh and the last vow, they promise that they would be true and loyal to each other and would remain companions and best of friends for the lifetime.

I closed my eyes for a moment as I wished that moment to come soon for us.

'You are sleeping Anuj,' she removed ash from my shoulder, which came from the *havan khund*.

'No…not sleeping, was lost somewhere,' I grinned and felt her touch when her cold hand touched my neck.

'Even if you want to sleep, you can't, sorry…,' she laughed. Her mother called her and she said to me, '*Beta* can you help her.'

'Sure aunty,' I replied.

'May I help you ma'am,' I said from the door.

'Hey, why you are here?' Pakhi said.

'My mother-in-law told me to help you,' I teased her.

'Yes, of course. So funny, shut up and hold this,' she turned and pointed to a heavy bag in the corner of the room. I came to the window side and looked at the heavy bag. I bent down to hold that bag, and at the next moment, cold fire ran into my body. She hugged me from the back tightly. Her hands were around my neck, her left cheek was on my left side of the shoulder and I could feel her warmth. Lights were dim, hands were dusty but one thing was clear, her love. I turned back to her and looked into her eyes. Her hands were around my waist now, and her waist touched mine.

'What happened?' I pushed her closer.

'I hate you,' she pushed me tightly to her waist as much as she could. I moved my one hand up to her cheeks and second on her back.

'Whatever you are trying to do, I'll die for sure,' we hugged tightly. I murmured into her ears.

'I won't leave you now, I love you.'

'Someone will come. Let's go.'

'I don't want to go.'

'Don't be mad, let's go,' I said.

'Do you love me?'

'I love you and why not, you have a perfect figure that I could just feel.'

'I'll kill you,' she pushed me away.

We left.

I slept wherever I got place keeping that fire in me for some other moment.

Next morning when I was in sleep, I heard footsteps coming to my bed. I opened my eyes.

'Get up, get up,' Pakhi said.

'I don't know when I slept,' I replied.

'It's 5:30am now, getup,' she took my sheet and gave me a water bottle and offered me a bowl, 'Do you want *jalebi*?'

'Yes, I am feeling hungry,' I grinned and stood up.

She gave me a piece of *jalebi*, pushing a big piece of it in my mouth.

'Hmm…Hmmm…Wait…,' I could say nothing.

If *mehndi* gives a dark color on hands that shows the love of mother-in-law.

'Your mother-in-law loves you so much,' I touched her finger and smelled *mehndi* in her hands.

'And how do you know?' she bent her finger and locked with mine and wiped my mouth full of *jalebi*.

'Your *mehndi* says that,' I smiled and bit her finger.

'So funny, I'll cut you into pieces now and you'll get nothing,' she released herself.

'I love you,' my feelings made the moment adorable.

'Get lost,' she kicked me.

'I am not kidding, I love you a lot,' I became more romantic and licked her finger. She came close to me. My lips touched her forehead and she poured love in her eyes and closed them and locked her finger into mine.

'I'll miss you,' I said coming close to her ear. She started breathing fast. Her warmth forced me to come close to her and I moved ahead, she moaned and then her hand started rolling in my shirt.

'Is it good? Is this fine?' For a moment, I thought and then my heart said, 'Who cares.' The moment seemed as beautiful as I ever dreamt. She placed her head on my shoulder while running her hand in my hair, 'Don't leave me, I can't think my life without you, you have made my life happy and gave me a purpose to live. You have filled colors in it. Never go away.'

We both wanted to live that moment forever. I looked into her eyes, I could touch her, feel her and then suddenly I thought about that mail which was sent to Ajay. Tears came in my eyes with no reasons.

'Hey what happened,' she asked, kissing on teardrops. She touched her soft fingers on my lips. I forgot everything, held her hand tightly. The way she loved me, I didn't want to ask anything which could hamper out bonding. Her cheeks were wet and her hair went un-tied. She looked so pretty when few springs of hair touched her cheeks. She rolled them with her fingers. Her lips were deep red without any lip-gloss now and I just wanted to be with her forever.

'I'm always with you.' I promised her. She was holding my hands, brushing my arm and adjusting my hair. Then she placed her palm and head on my chest. We spent some time with no movements and then I set her bra strap. Being notorious, she poked her in my stomach. After that, she got busy in the exodus ceremony of bride and groom with her mother, and left in the noon.

Unofficially Yours

Surprises are not permanent else they would lose their existence but those are just to make your loved one feel special.

I wanted to plan a surprise party just for her. From last one week I was staying at my friend's place and I got an idea to plan something. An extremely spaciously large and wide room, painted with light relaxing colors and a big bay window, with lacy curtains, puffing down the sides. The furnishings were soft yet firm and ensured comfort in a spacious manor. The room had some weird smell. I used body deodorant to make it little sweet. A coffee table with some armchairs stood at the corner of the room with a stool next to it and few candles with matchsticks. A small LCD was kept next to the stool attached to the window. There were a couple of beautiful lead crystals on each of the two bedside tables with artwork on the walls. I made the room perfect and it looked so serene, it just screamed romantic and relaxing. I kept her favourite chocolates, wrapped in heart shaped earthy colored boxes all over the room. Some were under the pillow, some at the all four corners of the bed with different romantic messages. I put candles around the bed in series. After spending the whole morning I got a cake. There was no special occasion but I wanted to celebrate with no reasons.

It was 11:30 in the morning when I called her, 'Where have you reached?'

'Just coming, I don't know where you are staying, where will I come?' she questioned and added in some confusion, 'Would it look good to come at your place? I mean your friend, what will he think?'

'There is no problem in that. He is my nappy buddy and he knows about you. So you can come here,' I assured her.

She reached Noida sector-18 metro station. I waved my hand and messaged my friend Rohan- She is coming, in 5 minutes, lit the candles after two or three minutes.

Rohan was doing engineering from IIT-D and he was staying at Noida. I met him first time in our college two years back and from that day we were good friends, rather I would say sensible friends. I always asked him to which he would always reply- *I love travelling.*

Weird isn't it? Even I thought so but when he came to my college for fest last month, he proved that he was intelligent, funny, kind, compassionate, strong, a leader but not mean. He was loyal to everyone, honest, had a good career valued life and his health. He wasn't a drug addicted like others, he liked to travel around, loved to read. He had respect for different religions and sexual orientations. I can't say anything about his body type because that didn't really matter to him. He used to say- our mind works and body only works in bed not in gym. I knew, he was joking.

We walked for few minutes and then reached the place. We went upstairs, on the first floor. In front of the door, I bent down and pretended to tie my shoe laces because I wanted her to open the door.

'Hey! Can you open the door?' I asked her.

She opened the door. She was shocked, her mouth corners pointed in the different direction, in a lopsided smile, she looked at me, 'What is that? Don't tell me it's for me, I can't believe it.'

I smiled and poured more love in my eyes, 'Just for you.'

We entered; room was decorated with balloons and candles. A series of candles were placed at all three sides of the bed. One side had an open way to come to bed to cut the cake which was on the centre of the bed, poked with a small red candle on it. Candles in series were spreading light but that was enough to recognize our faces only. That made the moment more romantic. Dim lights, multi colored ribbons and balloons were polishing the beauty of the room. Candles seemed like stars, ribbons and balloons were dancing slowly with a light background song 'Hero' by Enrique and that video was playing on my laptop. Just like it usually happens in Hollywood movies. Awesome synchronization of her pictures with music.

We all greeted each other and then Rohan came to me secretly and said, 'It looks like a honeymoon bed, good job with candles, ribbons and balloons. Hope you could buy few roses too.'

'Yeah I wish I could but that's okay, next time,' I smiled and got busy with my special guest.

There were three more creatures when I entered; Akula, Gautami and Akarsh. I met them few days back and if I go with the calculations, they were two couples- Rohan – Akula and Akarsh – Gautami. I didn't know much about them but they were very kind and generous.

We all sat on the bed, ribbons and balloons were touching her cheeks where she was sitting. Green, red, blue balloons with multicolored ribbons and her soft cheeks just took my heart away.

'You are looking pretty,' Akula said and then looked at me. I just smiled. She tried to make me blush, it seemed that I already was blushing when I saw Pakhi so happy.

Akarsh said, 'Let's cut the cake, come Pakhi.'

'Oh chocolate cake, I want it full,' she made everyone laugh.

'You are already very healthy,' I teased her.

'Look at you, skeleton,' she laughed turning to me with a knife and blinked with an airy kiss.

'I am ready to die from your hands,' I murmured.

She blew out the candle and poked the knife into the cake, everybody clapped for the celebration and we considered it as the celebration of her birthday that we couldn't celebrate earlier.

Eyes fluttering, a naughty smile on her face, she pasted the big piece of cake on my face and laughed like a devil. I was just paused for a minute, looked at everybody and everybody laughed at me. This wasn't funny because my eyes were having full of cream.

'Don't waste the cake on my face,' being very decent I said and took a piece of cake and touched her mouth however, at the next moment I wasn't in a mood to fail at this battle and pasted all the cream on her face and laughed as much as I could. I also knew how to be funny though I got few harsh kicks but that was okay. We enjoyed the birthday celebration followed by a funny lunch with weird jokes as pickle with every bite of it. Though we had met many times before but it was like I was at home with her.

Pakhi was showing the burning candle to balloons and enjoying recoils of its blasting. It was afternoon when everybody started leaving the place as they had to go.

'Are you staying here or going anywhere?' Rohan asked. I didn't answer and then he continued, 'If you are staying here, leave these keys on that meter when you leave,' showed finger to the electronic meter which wasn't running it seemed.

'No, we are just leaving,' Pakhi replied with slow voice as she wasn't comfortable to stay alone. There are some senses we all carry and girls are best in them. Not to allow anyone to make any judgments, she said so. We also left while others already left. We came downstairs. We could only walk few steps.

'Can't we stay for some time at the room?' I didn't look at her, just touched her palm with my fingers while walking.

Even she didn't look at me, and just gave a soft touch on my fingers and suddenly removed, I said, 'Let's go. I'm tired.'

'No, we'll go to TGIP mall, I have to buy a bag and you are going to help me, okay.'

I wanted to spend some time with her alone. I wanted to feel her alone. I wanted to love her alone. She showed her ignorance.

After looking at my innocent face, she said, 'You guys just want to stay with a girl alone, isn't it?'

'It's nothing like that. We will go for shopping now,' I smiled and started following her footsteps.

'Crazy fellow, it's hot outside we'll go for shopping in the evening. Even I am feeling tired. If you make coffee for me, then I can stay for some time,' she grinned.

'That I am ready to make for the rest of my life.'

We turned back and reached at the gate. There was junk shop just opposite to the entrance of the flat. A tall man with long beard; both hands full of dust; his eyes were red, I guessed he was drunk. He looked at me as if I had stabbed him. I ignored his gesture and came to Pakhi's right side to hide her from his bad sight. We moved upstairs. The keys were on the electronic meter, which were covered with a piece of paper. I unlocked the room and we entered.

Two or three candles were still spreading the light in the room. I switched on the lights. She looked tired and thirsty.

'You sit here and lock the room; I will just come,' I moved outside the door.

'Where are you going?' she stood a bit to stop me. She felt scared and even more after seeing that weird man outside.

'Hey I will just go and get a water bottle. You lock the door from inside,' I checked. I came downstairs and shouted at that man, 'Any problem you have? Have you never seen any girl in your life, you jerk?' He didn't speak.

I bought the water bottle and came back. I knocked the door while breaking the seal of the water bottle, 'Hey open the door. It's me, Anuj.'

She opened the door. Firstly, I gave her the water bottle. I looked at her dress, white T-shirt with blue denim. She was looking pretty. She gulped down half the bottle in one go. Her lips were wet now. She took a last sip of water and kept the bottle on the stool. My laptop was on the corner of the bed. She played a romantic song; that made the moment more beautiful, I liked it and then...

Unhooked, Removed & Exchanged

I looked into her beautiful eyes. Suddenly she blinked her eyes. I shivered for a moment as I had the best girl in my life. Life seemed so complete.

'What are you thinking?' Pakhi dragged herself to me and asked.

'Nothing,' I smiled and I never wanted to tell how much I loved her, I just wanted to make her feel every moment, 'By the way, I have something for you,' I continued.

'Oh really, for me, was this not enough what you did, is this a dream, someone pinch me,' she looked excited and lovely. I took the box that I hid last night under the bed. She opened the box and it was thigh length sleeve less black night wear with red border. 'Are you sure, it's for me?' she asked but she was confused. She actually loved it.

'I got this for you. I can't be with you every night in bed but this will love you whole night whenever you'll miss me,' I touched the dress and could feel her happiness from it, 'And you can feel my touch anywhere you want,' I laughed.

'Shut up you bugger,' she punched on my shoulder and kissed on my hands. We didn't speak for a moment and then she looked at me, 'Should I try this out here?'

'This entire place is yours. You are always welcome, if you want to try. I'd like to see you in this dress.'

'Actually you aren't supposed to see me in this dress before marriage,' she grinned.

'We've done many things before marriage, so this is just a formality,' I blinked at her. She went to the other room, 'You're the craziest fellow I have ever met in my life.'

'You won't find any other, don't worry,' I laughed and took a sip of orange juice from the glass.

She emerged from the room in a while. She was standing at the door with an air of carefree confidence that took all my attention because the dress was absolutely fit on her. I couldn't ignore her curves and moves when she covered few more steps towards me. She was comfortable with herself. Her wry smile across a smoke filled room made me smile. Wondrous oceans of gaze out in playful curiosity as she asked, 'How am I looking?' I was just stunned. Though, I could see hint of a wild spark lingering behind those lids but I left it on her to take the opportunity this time. She herself came to me and asked again the same question, 'How do I look in this?'

'I really shouldn't speak anything now,' I took her to bed and threw. She started shouting with weird acts, 'No, I'll kill you.'

We hugged each other and I murmured into her ears, 'You look amazing, this fits perfectly.'

'So you wouldn't want to remove this from my body and I'm safe today,' she teased me and turned to the other side on the bed. It was too soon and I felt awkward so preferred to dance with her, 'Hey, you know I just love this song. Would you like to dance with me?'

She shrugged her shoulders. Her charcoal eyes met mine again. I smiled and gave a brief nod. That was the best time to romance with her with perfect music and perfect time.

'Oh, with you…' She laughed, 'Do you really dance?' Now her dress filled all the loose spaces on her body and her body was giving the perfect response to the beautiful dress. I was too eager to hug her once. She was looking stunning.

'Yes, I can do belly dancing for you,' pouring love in my eyes, I offered my hand to hold and invited her for dance.

'I would prefer to go for Salsa,' I pulled her towards me and placed her hand on my back and other on my shoulder. Before she could dominate, I locked her hand which was on my back and pulled her to me taking one round around.

'You're not bad in salsa, so with how many girls have you done this before?' she asked and I know that her actual question was, with how many girls I had done this.

'Only you can correct my moves which I think I'm skipping right now, nobody else can even afford doing it, so it's happening first time with me, and if you want to know the actual count then I danced so many times in my dreams, more than ten times.' We were just shaking our bodies with each other.

'So what did you do after dancing in your dreams?' she asked. I held her tightly from her waist and looked into her eyes, 'I take you to bed and kiss you.' She had so many expectations in her eyes and she was ready to make them come true.

'So can we make those dreams come true today?' she kissed on my lips softly. We went deep with very next second without giving any second thought in mind. It felt so beautiful, so soft and pleasurable.

'Take me to the bed,' she gave a gaze. Things were just moving smoothly; she placed her neck my shoulder on the bed. I touched her fish shaped earrings then gave a soft gentle touch on her neck. We both were lying on the bed, looking at the ceiling, filling colors in dreams. Happiness is when you dream together, make them true together and live together with those dreams. I kept my index finger on her lips, 'I love you, and I just want to love you forever.'

'I love you too.' She became more comfortable in my arms. I held her hand and placed one hand on her shoulder, other on her cheeks and pulled her to my side gently. She looked at me with sharp sight and hypnotized me for seconds. I swept my hand over her head and kissed on her forehead. 'What are you doing?' I kissed on her lips without mentioning anything. I laid on her and covered her full body with mine. I came close to her face and sensed her warmth. One hand on her neck and other just below, I took a big bite on her lips two three times deeply and she responded with the same passion. 'Hey switch off the lights,' she whispered. At these moments hands work faster than anything. I jumped out of the bed and switched off the lights and came back. It was completely dark in the room and that nightdress suited her perfectly. I started kissing and went along with the border of the dress. From shoulder to thighs I could smell her body, My hand went to her shoulder and moved inside a bit. She laughed and removed my hand, 'Anuj shut up, it's tickling.' Then I moved to the stomach and kissed, 'I love this.'

'You always had a wish to eat pastry on my stomach; would you like to have cake on it?' I didn't speak anything and turned her down on the bed. I took a big piece of cake from the table and put it on her back.

'It's cold,' she shook from her waist. Before she could speak more, I took a small bit of cake along with the fragrance of her body from her back. I enjoyed each bite of it. She didn't speak, just moaned and felt good. I grabbed courage and gently put my whole palm a bit up to fell the softness of her body. 'Anuj! Remove your hand,' she held my hand tightly to move and then in a while her hand gave support to be there for some time. I smiled and responded by claiming her lips with a passionate kiss. She responded more than four times the pace I had.

'You're too fast,' I unhooked the hooks of her dress and she started loving me madly. Laces were still tied, I pushed her back but then suddenly, she locked my lower lip with both her lips. She didn't just love, she owned me. She won the battle of kisses and I never wanted lose it easily. This playful moment took us in a different world and we never wanted to come out of it. I wanted to hold this moment forever with a girl with whom I was going to spend my life. The picture of her as my life-partner flashed. She turned and laid on me. We rolled in bed several times. I placed my hand on her waist and other moved in her top to the neck. Before my hand reached her, she gripped my hand hard. I kissed her again so deep, then jerkily she pushed my hand inside and upper hand could feel her maturity.

'Are we going to fast?' she whispered and locked me in her arms and came on my?

'Do you think so?' I responded.

'No.'

I kissed on her shoulder, 'I love this dress.' I bit there softly. 'I want to see the brand of your inner-wears. May I take off this beautiful dress?' her hands ran on my back the moment I asked. She grinned and moments didn't allow us to stop, 'Yeah, you can.' She nodded and licked her lower and upper lip consecutively. I took one lace of her dress and opened it. She closed her eyes and I kissed on her back, 'You are beautiful,' I whispered.

'Don't be mad,' she tried to oppose me; I licked her neck and then a bit below. My hands didn't take much time to open her dress completely and she did the same with the button of my denims. I caressed her breast and she started responding to my pace, and then synchronized. She stretched her hands and I took off her dress. Both the bodies touched and we merged into each other. The moments were wet with desire and our intentions were not good. It's embarrassing to tell a girl to take off your pants. She shoved her hand in my pants. Two bodies can't have same temperature, doesn't matter how much fire you have for your love. Her touch was cold but now her acts were enough to take me higher with all the fire. I unhooked her bra. It was tight but practice makes a man perfect and I did it. She pinched me on my waist.

'Ahh, why are you pinching me?' I almost shouted. She kept her hand on my mouth, 'I didn't pinch you.' I threw the denim from my legs to the other side of the bed and she sat on my waist. She took a long breath and shook her head, without making any eye contact with me. She placed her both palms on my neck and put her teeth on my neck to give a love bite as she promised. She started kissing passionately on my chest and sucked and moved to the stomach.

'Oh shit, what happened?' she got up.

'What happened,' I asked.

'You are bleeding,' she got confused and looked at my legs, and continued, 'Did you lose your virginity?'

'That I lost so many days before,' I laughed.

'Shut up, bed sheet is all red,' she looked worried. I turned and saw that the knife which was used to cut the cake had put a cut on my waist.

'Oh shit,' I threw the knife on the table.

'Do you have cotton or Dettol?' she asked, still worried about the red bed sheet.

'I don't know.'

'Betadine?'

'Must be in the fridge,' I laughed.

'I'm not joking,' she tried to release herself.

'I don't live here; I don't know where it is. It's okay, it was plastic knife,' I pulled her to me.

'You're mad,' she went to the waist and licked, she looked up to my eyes, 'Is it paining?'

'Of course not,' I pampered on her head. She licked for almost a minute, and all the blood and pain went away. I turned her back and unbuttoned her jeans. She tried to grip but passion overruled everything. My legs touched her legs; she shivered, took a long breath. She came on me, tried to cover my body with her legs and rubbed her tongue on my chest to stomach. I was setting her hair, and she went low, bit low, and bit low. I closed my eyes and lost myself in her love. 'You're amazing.'

She looked at me, her chin was on my stomach, and her sight was sharp, she smiled in her notorious way.

'Did you feel good?'

'Yeah,' I pulled her up to my face. I could feel her warmth. She kissed gently on my lips, moved my hand under her jeans and now she closed her eyes. I felt something warm and went ahead and put my hand as deep as I could. I pushed my waist to her waist and then she pushed with the same force. This went for some time until she gave few hard strokes on my waist and then seemed calm.

'Did you like this?' I asked, covering her with my arms. She almost moaned and replied, 'Yes baby, and I missed you a lot.' Cell phone vibrated.

'Where is my cell phone, its ringing' locking her small fingers into mine, I asked.

'Hey, it's here, but mine is ringing. Just keep quiet, mom is calling.' She picked the call, 'Hello.'

'Nothing just came for shopping with my friend,' she looked at me. She was still on the bed, no clothes on her body and same with me. hugged her from back. She pushed me back.

'Yes mom, I'll reach home by 3 or 3:30, okay mom bye,' she disconnected. I was kissing on her back and rubbing my tongue on her shoulder.

'Anuj, get up, we need to leave now,' she stood up a little, covered herself with the bed sheet. She wore inner-wears and t-shirt. She picked her other clothes and went to the washroom.

'Hey, it's my t-shirt you wore,' I said.

'Let me change, till that time stay naked,' she laughed and moved. I searched for the rest of my clothes. They were all over the place. She entered the room.

'Hey hey, at least knock before entering,' I was just wearing the clothes but almost naked.

She laughed, 'And what was happening few minutes back, now I know all your measurements,' she teased me and laughed. She switched on the lights. Her cheeks were red and lips seemed tired. She went in front of mirror and set her hair with both her hands. She said decisively, 'I have to go home.'

'It's only 2:55. Take rest for some time and then I'll drop you,' I pointed to the tableside clock.

She nodded.

We closed our eyes for some time.

She pushed me hard, 'Anuj, get up, it's 4:30, and I have to go home. Mom called me six times.' She looked tensed now.

I didn't speak and I just got ready in next two minutes without having a face wash. Luckily we got the metro on time and I dropped her at her nearest metro station. I waved to say good bye and she left.

If I could go Back

After a week when I was sitting in the examination hall, I received a message, my phone was on silent mode but only messages could give multiple vibrations. I actually kept those settings to know instantly if she messaged me. I looked around hiding myself from six faculties from each corner.

```
My papa left me forever, just because of you.
I hate you.
You stopped me to go home that day when mamma
called me. If I could leave, I could have met
him one last time. He was in the hospital that
day. I won't forgive you in my life. Just go
away and never show your face. You just wanted
to come close to me and you got that. Now, just
go away from my life. Just go away!
```

I didn't know what to do. I submitted my answer sheet and ran to the hostel. I just walked into the washroom. I felt split into pieces. I started massaging my forehead and temples but the pain persisted and my body started hurting and itching. I wasn't crying and I couldn't cry. I just needed someone to tell me what to do but nobody was there. My nose started bleeding and the blood ran down to neck. I stood for a couple of seconds but my stomach was churning and eyes were closed. I just pressed them so hard. I wanted to crawl into someone's lap and then at the next moment I stood up and ran to the exit gate of the college with a small bag, phone charger and wallet. I didn't want to call her after what happened. My face was pale and body was lethargic. Changing trains and buses I reached Delhi early morning and just messaged her to know where I could come. She just sent me the address of the cremation place where they were taking the body. I reached there directly.

I was standing there and I had no senses. I could only try to go and meet her but she didn't respond and ignored me. Everybody left and I tried to stop her after the cremation to talk to her.

'I don't want to meet you and please stop following me and leave me forever. You got what you wanted, now go away,' she burst out and left. Her brother asked her, 'Is there any problem?' She didn't respond and they all left.

I just dropped her a message and came back to college-

```
I can't get your days back to you but I am always
with you. Take care of your mom and yourself,
she needs you. I love you. You will make things
better. Don't lose yourself.
```

She left for her hometown. Days passed, weeks passed and a month passed, we started talking over the phone, once or twice in a day.

She called me after a month when she reached Delhi.

'Are you in Delhi?' I asked her.

'No, reaching in few minutes, you say, how are you?' she asked me. Those words were just enough for me.

'I am fine, you just come and take rest, you must be tired,' I said.

'Yeah, reaching, just stuck in traffic,' she said.

It seemed we were again back to the initial days when I used to find reasons to talk to her. Slowly and steadily, we again started our journey but it was hard to skip those hurdles which already had been given to us.

She started going to college. I tried to make her life normal and easier as it was earlier but many things were changed. I tried to do everything for her but I could only give her moral support.

We always talk about moral support and wishes but the fact is, we as a human need someone physically to listen. I wasn't in front of her and she missed me at those moments. Months passed, she started living her life normally. I made her laugh and things started coming back on the right track.

Happiness is
when I am with you

It was beginning of 2011 when we all were running to get a good job with a decent salary package to in-cash the amount we spent on our education.

We both had plans to go to Mumbai and now I couldn't go there. She wanted to join NIMS for MBA and I had to start my life after getting a good job. Her best friend Neha was there in Mumbai and she was excited to meet.

This was an important day for me. I was getting ready for the interview with one of the most prominent companies in Jaypee, Noida, as we had centralize placement cell there. All students from Jaypee group colleges across India had to come to Noida for their dream jobs.

'Hey, are you sure you'll get Mumbai as your job location?' she asked.

'I hope, else let's see. We will manage,' I replied, sitting in a conference hall, filling details in a form as I had already cleared the written aptitude test.

'Hey listen, I have to fill three preference locations,' I asked her over the call.

'Okay, first fill Mumbai, second Pune because if you don't get Mumbai, at least we can meet over the weekends.'

'And third?'

'Is it required to fill the third?' she asked in confusion.

'Yes, else they will send me to Chennai.'

'Then you can fill Delhi, to be on the safer side.'

'Hope I'll get my first preference Mumbai, I love you, bye. I need to go for the interview,' I disconnected.

A black file in my left hand; pen in my pocket, college tie, everything perfect, I looked like a complete man. However, I was nervous, not because I was going for an interview, but just because I badly wanted the work location to be Mumbai, also because of some others questions.

'What if I am not selected?'

'What will they think about me?'

'I have spent enough and now I have to crack this interview, anyhow.'

Indian families actually expect a lot from their children, that I realized the moment I entered the interview hall. If you want to do something different, it doesn't matter because they won't allow you anything except 'Engineering' or 'Medical.' You'll be either an engineer or a doctor. My mind was still remembering all those courses, formulas, networking, electronics, programming and a lot more. These questions started making me nervous; anyhow, I controlled and thought, 'Just clear the interview and then you will get the ticket to Mumbai...THE DREAM PLACE,' I smiled.

'May I come in sir,' I looked for an approval to enter the interview room.

'Yes, please come, sit,' The technical person looked at me and smiled.

'How are you Anuj?'

'I am fine. Thanks.'

I was expecting a young lady in the interview room, a cute face, dimples and cute smile as my seniors told me but nothing happened like that. He was forty years old, I guessed. Dark black hair, moustaches, surely he dyed his moustaches. I wanted to smile but I couldn't because he was my…DESTINY.

'Anuj if you'll laugh today, your destiny will laugh at you for the rest of your life,' I didn't do any stupidity.

'Have your seat Anuj,' he said, looking at my pen, which I kept in the pocket of my blazer. I sat in the chair, and put my interview file on the table in front of the interviewer. Interviewer looked at the interview file; I dragged a bit to his side. Eyes were on the file; he was turning the mark sheets of my every semester and then again went back to my CV to look at my achievements. I was happy when he looked at my achievements, 'I am good in studies and extracurricular activities so I'm cleared,' I thought.

Then a question came form that end, 'So tell me something about yourself?'

I was just waiting for this question. This was a universal question that was asked in all the companies. I was well prepared for this and gave my best shot at it. He stopped me in the middle and asked few very technical questions that I answered correctly and few wrongly but with confidence.

Happily I completed technical round but this was not over, I had to clear one more round of HR interview.

'Now you'd be selected, as HR is a lady,' one of my friends said.

'Let's see. I am nervous,' I entered.

After moral formalities, the HR lady asked me just one question, looking at my form, 'You are from Bareilly, I have taken so many interviews till now, everybody wants working location as Delhi and you are the first person giving interview here and wanting to go to Mumbai, any specific reasons?'

I smiled, 'Ma'am as such there are no specific reasons but I chose Mumbai because I can come to Delhi anytime but now is the time when I can explore the other places and it's not far away from Delhi. Moreover this is the age when I can learn.'

The HR lady smiled, 'Okay, nice, we want guys like you who are flexible in shifting to locations. Hope you'll get it.' She asked few more questions about me, my family, about the company.

I was training and placement coordinator and I could easily check my result before it was declared officially. I just called my mom to give her this good news that her son did what she expected from him... ONE MORE ENGINEER.

This is what Nobody Wants

```
There  is  no  importance  of  sweetness  without
sour.
There is no importance of good without bad.
There is no importance of smile without tears.
There is no life without fate but one thing is
above all…LOVE and that makes you great.
```

Now I was an engineer, officially, with a respectable package. So I stopped counting money. At least in the initial few year, until I got married perhaps. So, I booked three seats while going for the movie. Two for us, and one to make space between us and others.

'When he holds my hand, I feel like he is my true friend,' she said, sitting in theatre, looking at the screen. Her line sliced me. I asked 'Who?'

'Arpan, he's a good guy,' she said.

'Hm good.'

'What hmm, feeling jealous,' she said with trembling chin.

'No…I am not,' I smiled, jaw put forward.

'Hey, you know, he dropped me on bike few days back and after a long time I felt happy. Suddenly it started raining and then he asked if he could drop me,' she said very normally but that was not normal for me, it was enough to be a murderer of that guy. I didn't have to be over possessive, so controlled myself from speaking any stupid thing that could hurt her. She felt good and that was enough for me.

'He dropped you on bike?' I asked, flared nostrils.

'It's nothing like that?' she answered.

'Nothing, but that's not good, well you know what is right or wrong,'

'I was getting late so...'

'It's okay. He holds your hand, drops you at metro station on bike, it's okay, but does he know you are committed?'

'Does it really matter to tell everyone that we're in a relationship? He knows, you are my good friend and when my papa passed away then he was the only one who supported me, he made me happy, whenever I felt bad. You were not here those days Anuj. He is just my friend.'

'I know it's not wrong, I trust you but what if he likes you. And why don't you tell him that you are committed with me, I know guys, why to give any hopes to anyone for any problem in future?'

'Why don't you trust me, he is just my friend,' she reacted.

'But why do you hide our relationship from others, just tell me why? Don't you love me?'

'I love you but I don't want to tell, please trust me.'

'You do wrong and then you expect me to accept that.'

'Anuj, if you don't trust me then why are we in relationship?'

'What did you say?' I asked.

'Why are we in this relation, if you don't trust me,' she repeated.

'Hmm...fine, I knew that, you never loved me, thanks for everything.'

'Hey, why are you crying? It's nothing like that, I love you a lot. I just want you to trust me,' she held my hand and I too held her hand tightly and put my head on her shoulder. She had changed from the day her father passed away. She stopped talking about our future. She was broken but I was trying to bring our old days back.

Next week it was 14th February, Valentine's Day. I asked her a day before to meet and then she said, 'Is it important to show off our love.

Moreover, Shivsena roams around Noida and Delhi on Valentine's Day, so we'll meet on 15th,' she almost refused to meet.

However, I knew what I was; I wanted to meet her that means I had to meet her, no matter where I was. It was a special day for me. I woke up early in the morning at six. I just ran outside in search of a flower, as I wanted to buy few roses for her with fish shaped earrings that I got last night after visiting almost all the shops of CSM and TGIP mall.

I bought one red rose from the metro station, and shoved in my pocket of shirt to keep it fresh and then wore blazer because after that I had to reach Jaypee College, Noida for some placement activity.

I called her, 'Hi, good morning! Happy Valentine's Day, I love you sweetie.'

'Can we meet for five minutes,' I requested, excitement was in my voice.

'Can you come at CP metro station, just for five minutes?'

'I'm getting late for college,' she replied.

'Okay you go, I'll see you at Kashmiri gate, okay?' I tried another way to meet her.

'You don't come at Kashmiri gate, my friends are waiting over there so it's not possible to meet. We can meet tomorrow,' she replied.

My plan was almost over and I looked at the pocket under the blazer. I touched that red rose, felt bad but I thought these were the moments to prove. I charged up and checked my watch. I called her again, 'Where are you now?' I was running on the platform to catch the next metro as soon as possible.

'I have reached Kashmiri gate metro station and where are you?' she replied. I had reached CP which was just two-three stations before.

'I am at CP,' my voice grunted due to network issues. I was in a hurry.

'I'm getting late, we'll meet tomorrow okay, I'm going.' She disconnected or it was disconnected due to network but it seemed for her it was just like a normal day but I had waited for this for long.

Someone pushed me, '*Abey dikhai nhi deta kya?*'

'Sorry.'

'What sorry?'

'Shut up, I pushed you because someone pushed me, now better shut your mouth,' I shouted, people in the metro looked at me.

'What are you doing Anuj, talk to you later, It's not possible to meet now.'

'Okay, you go,' my voice low; eyes red and started getting wet from her reply, frustrated, I de-boarded the metro at the next station and I came back.

I looked at my wristwatch and then at the station clock, wiped my tears, sniffed and cursed myself, 'I was late, that's why I couldn't meet her, I'm the culprit.'

'Did she deserve me or am I so bad, if not then why does all this happen with me?' I felt helpless, wanted to sit for some time and cry.

```
The more you love, the more you cry, I don't
know why.
For you I run, for you I cry,
For you my love, everything I try,
Your smile makes me happy; your tears make me
sad,
Your absence makes me unhappy and I feel like
dead,
I actually feel bad; I don't want to lie,
Your love makes me happy; your loves make me
cry, I don't know why.
```

I ran to the exit of CP metro station. I was already late and got auto rickshaw for college. Sitting and looking somewhere outside, I thought about all fights and that mail she sent to Ajay. I sniffed, rickshaw guy looked at me and I turned my face to the other side and didn't look at the front mirror for few minutes. I reached campus.

'Whenever I try to do something, she doesn't give me a chance,' I thought, dialling her number. She picked my call, 'I'm in class now, talk to you later.' Call disconnected. I messaged her- `I want to meet you if you have time for me. I know you are very busy but please inform me, whenever you are free.`

My phone flashed the arrival of her message-

`I'm in college, attending all classes, I'll b free in the evening because there is an extra class. I'll not able to meet you. We'll meet later.`

I had lost the earrings while coming from CP that I bought for her last night.

'Enough is enough, what the hell is she doing. If she was busy with her classes, at least she could talk to me for a while,' I was in pain and burst out.

I called her again, 'I have to meet you, just for five minutes, please come after college, I'll come wherever you want.'

'Why do you not understand I'm in the class, attending lectures, talk to you later,' she shouted this time.

'Okay sorry.' I decided not to call her. There is no alcoholic beverage stronger than love.

In the evening I got her text and she asked me to reach Ansal Plaza. Forgetting everything I just reached there.

'Anuj, this is not the way, why don't you understand? I was in college, and you were calling me again and again,' she was normal now and smiled.

'I missed you,' I said, blinked my eyes and gave that rose, 'Happy Valentine's Day. I love you.'

'For this rose you were irritating me since morning? Now I should go, I have a headache,' she responded normally but her words hurt me.

'You want some water?' I looked at her.

'No, I have to go.' I gave her water bottle, 'Have some water. You want chocolates?' I smiled looking at her dry face.

I always used to give her chocolates when we met.

'I don't want,' she replied, opening the cap of the bottle and took few more sips from it.

'Have it, you are getting late, you should go home,' I kissed on her hands.

'Please don't mind. But I can't keep this rose with me, if someone will see at home then it would be a problem for me,' she said, walking and moving to the exit of the mall. That rose I kept in the diary she gifted me, and it's still there. I waved my hand, when she left the mall.

```
Sometimes you never give a chance to forgive,
you just smile and hug them.
```

Anything to be with you

It was early spring of 2011 and I wanted to give surprise by reaching Delhi.

In train, hanging my phone as up as I could, I called her, 'Hey, I am coming to meet you.'

'What?' she was shocked.

'Talk to you later, I'm with my mami,' she disconnected the call. Few minutes later my phone vibrated with her message-

```
My friend Shruti is staying at my home today,
So, I'll not be able to come in the morning.
I will come around 1:00 pm if I could make it
possible.
```

Leaning on the wall of the train, I was thinking to find a way to meet her. I called her again, 'This isn't done Pakhi. You can't come on time and will you go to college?'

'Yes, I have some work, so will go to college. I'll see you after that,' she replied rudely. I lost my temper and became frustrated. I didn't call her for next two hours and when I did call her- *Your call is on wait, please stay on the line or call again later.* Again, I called after sometime- *Your call is on wait, please stay on the line or call again later.* I started calling her repeatedly. She picked my call and she disconnected after saying that, 'Anuj, please don't irritate me by calling again and again.' I thought she'd ask where had I reached but nothing happened like that because shit happens like that.

Early morning, I reached Delhi. She called me, 'Where are you, I'd be there by 1:00 pm. Can you come to Anand Vihar? We'll meet there.'

'Okay', I replied. I was staying at the same place where we met last time.

We went to Ansal Plaza which was near to Anand Vihar metro station. Unexpectedly, she asked me for movie. I guessed that was the best place to spend time with her.

'Yeah, sure,' I replied, looking at her, many questions were running in my mind, I wanted to ask with whom she was talking yesterday, to whom she mailed few months before, but didn't ask because I didn't want to spoil the things. We moved to the ticket counter and bought two tickets of F.A.L.T.U. We entered the theatre, seated on J-18 J-19. Now she was happy but I was not. Questions were still roaming in my mind. My eyes were on the screen but my mind was just thinking about fights, arguments and waiting calls. I ignored many times but something was wrong, I was sure but didn't have guts to ask because I didn't want to fight, didn't want to lose her.

Blandly she asked, 'Want to have something?' I replied looking at the screen, 'No.'

She came after 15 minutes. She was enjoying the movie and having snacks but I was silent. After 20-30 minutes, she held my hand and looked into my eyes and said, 'I love you.'

Those three words and I forgot everything. When she touched my chest, I lost my senses; when she kissed on my lips, I lost everything. I held her hand very tightly. I kissed on her hand. She kissed on my cheeks and I whispered into her ears, 'I lovee youuu...'

At the next moment Pakhi said, 'Why do you doubt on me?'

'I trust you baby, but when you say that is right while actually that's wrong, then? This isn't doubt, I trust you baby,' I said coming close to her neck.

Love was in her eyes, her voice pretty, sorrow in her few lines, she said, 'I am always with you. I'm not going anywhere. Arpan is just my friend nothing more than that. I just love you. But I don't feel good when you doubt on me.'

'Is he good looking?' I grinned, actually wanted to know about that bastard.

'No he looks like a girl, he's not even boyfriend type,' Pakhi said and I felt good, A GIRLY BOY...I laughed.

'Then what's your type?' I asked.

'Red and blue but not high cut briefs and braless, yes braless,' she laughed out loud. A couple sitting next to us looked at us.

'Hey, tell me, what's your type?' I again asked.

'A guy like you,' and she locked her lips with mine. She kissed me as hard as she wanted to do it from so long. We were into each other but I had to ask few things that troubled me from so long.

I replied, 'I don't doubt you Pakhi but I don't feel good when you talk to Arpan so much.'

'Whenever I talk to him, I tell you and I don't lie,' she said, leaving my hands, looking at the screen. She felt bad but that was truth, she lied some times. I asked, I wanted to hug and cry, why does she lie, 'Is Arpan more important than me?'

'It's not like that but my friendship is more important than love as I think at this point of time. I can't leave my friends,' she replied, her voice clear, no regret in her voice, as if she never did anything wrong in her life but this relationship. I was shocked and had no words.

'I'm not saying don't talk to your friends but why talk to Arpan so much. If you have feelings for him then tell me baby, I'll not ask you second time,' I said, putting courage in my heart.

'It's not like that, I love you and he is just my friend nothing more than that,' Pakhi said, she didn't look into my eyes and that made me uncomfortable.

'Pakhi, I have a question in my mind, we have completed more than two years with each other but none of your friends know about us. I know you are right and I always trust you but I don't know about others. If you talk to him as a friend so much, but he doesn't know that you are committed then might be he can take it in a wrong way? And I know guys better than you,' I tried to explain the truth.

Pakhi said, 'My friends are my everything, I can leave anything for them.'

'I am not saying Pakhi that you shouldn't talk to them but most of the time your number goes busy,' I replied, that most important question came out from my mouth.

She said, 'So that time you should stop calling me, when I'll be free I'll call you back for sure.'

'Again you are not accepting your mistakes. You do wrong things and say not to disturb. Do you want to leave me?' I felt bad and said something wrong in frustration.

She replied, 'Again you are doing the same thing, why should I leave you?'

She added, 'I am not doing anything wrong. You please forget the thing that I'm going to leave you. I just want to live my life. Why are you forcing me?'

I tried again, 'I am not forcing you baccha but this isn't right that you are committed with me and talking to another guy so much. I know you are right but you should understand that the other person can think in a wrong way…hm.'

Somewhere in my heart, I was still disturbed because nothing was resolved. I was confused; I was tired, I wanted to cry…IN HER ARMS and then…

Yes, I Cared

After watching the movie, we moved to Mahagun mall.

'What do you want and why are you doing this? Why are you hiding things?' once again, I asked the same question because those waiting calls blocked my mind. Pakhi ignored my questions and asked, 'You want something?'

I refused, 'No, I don't want anything.'

'I'll order *pani puri*, if you want, you can and stop thinking baseless things,' she smiled. She started enjoying *pani puri* and I was silent but angry, still stuck in those questions.

She asked me, 'Hey, do you have that song which you were singing in theatre.'

'Yes, I have,' I took her cell phone and was transferring the song, then an incoming call flashed on the screen. It was Arpan. Anger which I kept inside came on my face and I asked Pakhi, 'What's this?'

'Give me my cell phone,' she became conscious from my words.

'Sorry I can't give, at least I have this right to look into your cell phone,' I said and disconnected his call. I abused him from my heart, wished all things bad for him that I could think of. I checked her few messages; those messages were enough to influence my anger. Her phone flashed again, I disconnect again. She shouted at me, 'What are you doing with my cell phone, give me my phone, Anuj.'

I replied, all face muscles were frozen as in a mask, 'I won't give, sorry.' At the next moment, a message flashed on her cell phone's screen- What happened, pick my call sweetie.

The word 'sweetie' created so many problems within seconds in my mind. I just shouted and said, 'Pakhi, what's this? And what do you want?'

Pakhi replied as if this was a very normal thing for her, 'What happened, this is normal message. What's the problem?'

'Should I talk to him?' I warned her. She showed her anger, 'What nonsense, why are you creating a scene over here.'

'I am not creating any scene, you please tell me what's this,' I asked holding her phone in my hand. She stood up for water; I crossed my finger and mugged up Apran's number. This wasn't right or ethical but everything is fair in love and war. We left the restaurant and came out. I didn't give her phone because I wanted to talk and clear everything.

I said, 'Why are you not listening to me, where are you going, I have to talk, if you won't reply, I'll not give your cell phone.'

Sometimes you do wrong things to save your love but nobody looks at your right side.

I tried to stop her for next few minutes but she had only few words, 'I don't want to talk to you. I have to go. I'm getting late.'

She came to me and said, 'What do you want?'

'What do you want?' the same question I asked. She looked into my eyes and pleaded, 'I don't want anything. I have to go, I'm tired.' I looked into her eyes and requested, 'Please listen, what's this. This isn't fair. You don't care for me.'

'I care for you and I love you,' she smiled and her smile was enough to make me happy but not to resolve my problems or my anger.

We came out from the mall. She went home and I was completely alone without my unanswered questions. I called her after sometime, 'Pakhi, I love you but you do wrong things and then you say I'm doing right, it's not doubt, it's the very obvious thing and I want to be with you forever.'

She replied, 'Then you please don't call so much. We should give us some time. Let me miss you a little else we'll just fight.'

I was staying at Tilak Nagar at my friend's place and remembering all those promises which we made, when holding my hands she said, 'Never leave me alone, I can't manage all the things without you, you are my need, I love you like anything.'

I tried to feel her touch, remembered all those commitments and then lastly, that mail, which was sent to Ajay hit me.

It was 8:55 when phone flashed her call.

'Do you have my MAT form?' she asked in hurry.

Coming out from the room to balcony, I replied, 'No, I don't have. What happened?'

She asked me again, 'Check it in your bag. I must have kept it in your bag.'

'I don't have, you gave me that time and I returned it to you when we were sitting at Mahagun mall. You forgot again, right?'

I asked her, 'Should I go now?'

She didn't say anything and after a pause, she said, 'Tomorrow is the last day and I lost it at the last moment.

'Talk to you later. I will go and check,' I said and disconnected the phone line.

'Bro, I have to go it's urgent,' I apologized in front of my friend as I had some plans to go out with him.

'Anuj, this is not fair, you promised me,' he said, looking at me with half closed eyes.

I replied, wearing denim and t-shirt, 'I am really sorry yaar, please try to understand. I know we planned something but you don't worry I will come after some time.'

'But at this time, when will you reach there? The distance from here to Anand Vihar is more than an hour and then it will take some time to reach the mall. There is no use giving there at this time, moreover that mall closes at 10:00 pm, you can go tomorrow,' he added. I interrupted in between and requested, 'Please try to understand, it's really urgent I have to go.'

He grinned and replied, 'Seriously you are a crazy man! She made a mistake and now you are suffering.'

'She hasn't done anything. She usually forgets things, may be because of me,' I smiled and said, 'I'll be back after some time, and then we'll go to India Gate. I have to reach before 10:00 pm else…,' I smiled and ran the downstairs.

Looking at me his voice went low, 'It's not possible, but you can try, well come soon and take care.'

I shouted from the ground floor, 'At least I can try.'

It seemed impossible to reach on time if I waited for metro train. I asked rickshaw guys, 'Anand Vihar?'

He didn't reply for few seconds then he looked at me and said, 'Hm.'

'*Kitna loge*', I asked, looking at my watch. He was ready to make me fool and replied, 'Rs. 400.'

I requested, more like pleaded in front of him, '350 please?'

He said, '375 *isse kam nhi ho payega*.' I had only Rs. 350 in my pocket and then I collected all the coins from pocket and wallet and I could manage 369. I didn't tell and boarded the rickshaw. He looked at me when I was counting coins, he said, '375 *se kam nhi hoga*.' I de-boarded and he accelerated his rickshaw few steps ahead. 'Fuck you,' I shouted.

I decided to run to Tilak Nagar metro station to catch metro. I reached and ran to the escalator. Luckily, I stepped into the metro which was about to leave. I took a long breath. Now I was counting minutes and seconds that mattered. There were 18 to 20 stations between Tilak Nagar and Anand Vihar. I was calculating 3minutes/station and I calculated that I'll take an hour to reach Anand Vihar and then around 15 minutes from Anand Vihar metro station to Mahagun mall.

I dialled her number, '*Your call is on wait, please stay on the line or call again later.*'

'What the hell is going on,' I shouted in the metro. An aunty standing next to me looked at me. I lost my temper this time, 'I am running, trying everything for her and she is busy with someone else.' I remembered that message which I saw in the afternoon. My head started burning. I didn't think anything and dialled Arpan's number, '*Your call is on wait, please stay on the line or call again later.*'

The situation was worst now, I couldn't make myself a fool anymore that she was talking to someone else. Both of them were talking to each other, and that I had to accept. Few things cleared but I was waiting for her reply. Again, I called Pakhi, the same despondent sound into my ears and I again called Arpan after few minutes. He picked my call, 'Hello.'

I replied, once again I crossed my fingers, 'Hello! Hey, Is that Arpan? I'm Anuj.'

Arpan disconnected the line. At the next moment my phone rang, Pakhi called me, 'What happened; have you reached there?'

'To whom were you talking?' I asked in a breath and in an angry tone.

'I was talking to mom,' she replied very confidently. I disconnected the phone-line because she lied.

I called Arpan, biting my lips, my eyes squinted, 'Hi Arpan! Anuj here. I think you know me.'

He replied, 'Yeah, I know.'

Very politely, I asked about him. He asked about me, 'From where you are? What do you do?' Then I asked, 'Pakhi and I, we are in a relationship from almost years. You are Pakhi's friend, right?'

'Yes.'

'Arpan, I know you guys are good friends but things are not going fine and I respect your friendship. As a friend, you should help her. She is so irresponsible, she left her form and I'm in the metro going to search for it. I have a request; you talk to her but because of that we fight. I'm not saying that you should not talk to her. But please you should think about our relationship.'

Arpan understood what I wanted to say. He replied, 'Yeah, it's okay, I'll take care of it, don't worry. I'll not say anything to her.'

His last line 'I will not say anything to her,' I couldn't digest that. Pakhi was calling me repeatedly and then I picked her call, I said, 'I talked to Arpan.' She thought I was kidding. She didn't ask anything about it but I had the some questions, looking at the window and then at the route chart, I asked, 'Pakhi! What do you want and what are you doing, I really don't feel good.

'Don't irritate me Anuj, please; I'm not doing anything wrong.'

I asked her to clear everything, and again all face muscles were frozen as if in a mask, 'Then why did you lie?'

Pakhi replied, 'I wasn't lying and I'm not doing anything wrong, why do you always talk about Arpan. Arpan is just my friend, nothing more than that.'

'You know what is right or wrong and I love you because when you said for the first time, 'please never leave me', that day I had decided, I'll die but will never leave you. So take care next time, I trust you.' I looked at my wristwatch, it was 9:45 pm.

'I have just reached, talk to you later.' Call disconnected.

I was reaching Anand Vihar metro station.

I asked approaching the rickshaw guy '*Bhaiya Mahagun mall chaloge.*'

He was in sleep, looked into my eyes, 'Haannn...'

All the rickshaw guys were sleepy.

I didn't ask anything, sitting in the rickshaw, '*Bhaiya please jaldi chal.*' I ignored my wristwatch and looked at the CDMA cell phone watch, which said satellite timings, and watch said 10:05 pm.

'Fuck,' I said.

He turned to enquire that what happened.

'*Bhaiya thoda jaldi chala,*' I said to the rickshaw guy.

He replied with a nod, '*Chala toh raha hu, abhi five minutes aur lagenge.*'

While reaching near the entry gate I jumped out of the rickshaw and ran to the gate, and looked back, '*Wapis bhi jana hai.*'

He said, '*Bhaiaya kuch toh de do.*'

I gave him Rs. 100, 'Keep it, don't have change, wait here, I will just come.' I wished, looking at few couples that mall was still open. I ran on the escalators and reached on the second floor. I turned to the left side to find the same place where we were sitting in the afternoon. I found that restaurant and looked at the counter guy from whom Pakhi collected her order.

I recognized him. 'Sir, I left a form in the afternoon on that table.' I pointed to the exact table. He responded politely. All restaurant guys are polite or trained, I thought for a second.

'Yes, I have it.' He gave me the form and finally I took a long breath. Asked him for a glass of water and greeted him, 'Thank you so much sir, thank you so much.'

He smiled, 'You're welcome sir.'

'Thank you so much sir,' I said one more time, and left the restaurant.

Now I walked to the exit gate with a smile that I did it. I was looking for that rickshaw guy but I couldn't see him. He actually ran away with my 100 bucks.

'Bastard mofo,' I abused and hired another one for metro station. I called Pakhi and she picked my call, and before I could speak anything, she just asked, 'Did you get the form?'

I replied glibly, 'I enquired with the guy from him you took your order but he said there was no form there when we left the place.'

'How is it possible, we left it there only. Can you please check again? It would be there only.'

'But I checked there and there was no form in the lost and found section as well, he checked in my presence,' I said ingenuously.

'You didn't check properly, you please go back and check once again,' she said as she sniffed, 'I had to submit tomorrow, what I'll do now.'

'What are you saying? I checked and I got the form. When I'm with you, you should not worry,' I laughed and kissed her, coming close to the microphone, rickshaw guy tried to look at me but he must have known traffic rules and didn't look back.

What was my Mistake?

Next day I came back to my home. Though things were rough but I was pretty sure that I'd be able to make it as simple as they were before. I was sitting with my family at the dining table for lunch. She called me. I excused myself and received the call and angrily she asked, 'What did you do? You called Arpan, right? What did you think Anuj? You lied and showed your cheapness. I hate you, just hate you,' she shouted and felt like crying. 'Just get out from my life; I don't want to see your face in my life ever,' she made things complex.

I felt regret, why I did I call him? I wanted to make things normal, but had ended up making it worse.

'What happened!' pensively I asked.

'What happened, you have created problems for me. You have ruined my life and you are asking what did you do? Why do you want to break our friendship,' she just said what she wanted to.

'But Arpan knows about us, then what's the problem?' I asked, walking here and there in the lawn, looked inside from the window if someone could see me from the dining table.

'But I just told him that we are good friends, not in a relationship,' she replied aggressively.

'Pakhi you told me that Arpan knows about our relationship.' Things were getting worse with the way she started talking.

'Just shut up Anuj and please leave me alone, just get out from my life please. I don't want to see your face in my life ever,' Pakhi shouted very cheekily and repeated the same words.

'Don't say like this, I love you,' I tried to make the situation normal but she just kept on shouting. She disconnected the phone line. I tried her number again but she just said, 'I don't want to be with you anymore. I hate your cheap mentality, I hate your thinking, I just hate you, you always think wrong. Just get out from my life, please, don't ruin my life, please I beg of you please,' indignantly she said.

'Please don't talk like this, I really love you.' I was deeply hurt.

'But I hate you Anuj,' she disconnected the phone line.

I called her again- *your call is on wait, please stay on the line or call again later.*

I leaned on the wall; teardrops were wetting my cheeks and the floor.

I called her again, she picked my call, I asked, 'Talking to Arpan?'

'Yes,' Pakhi replied.

'When there is nothing like that then why are you doing all this?' I frowned.

'I am not doing anything wrong, you tried to ruin my life now please go away from my life.'

'Why are you talking like this?' I requested.

She shouted, 'Because I want to. A guy who doesn't trust me, how can I think my life with him?'

'I trust you...Please don't say like this.'

'Anuj, whatever it is but I don't want to talk to you.'

'Then why do you talk to Arpan so much,' I finally showed my anger after so much frustration. There is certain level to face things. I couldn't resist any more and busted out.

'It's my life, I haven't given any right to anybody to do this ok, so it's better you enjoy your life and please leave me alone.'

'Is it possible? I can't,' I said.

'I don't want to talk to you, now I don't see my future with you,' she wasn't listening what I wanted to convey.

'And what was going on from the last two years?'

Each and every day was perfect when we had good days and now time had turned back.

'I don't know,' she replied but she had no answer to give.

'Why don't you know? You know everything Pakhi, if you have feelings for someone else, then tell me, I promise you, I'll never talk to you, I'll never call you, but tell me at least.'

At some point of time I felt I was over reacting but there were few questions which had to be answered.

'Just shut up! I don't have feelings for anybody and this is the thing; I really hate your thinking and your irritating nature.'

'Yes, I am cheap. A girl who said- *don't leave me alone, I won't be able to live alone.* Now she is saying, get out from my life. Yes, I am cheap.' I added in a low voice with my one hand and head on the wall, 'Please don't call me.'

She disconnected. She was my need and I became mad for her. I left my friends, my studies, everything, and I just needed her in my life. My eyes were wet. To make her realize that I wasn't a cheap guy, I called her again but her number was still busy. They were talking to each other. I shouted, I kicked on the door, on the almirah and I kicked on the wall. I hit my head on the wall and it started bleeding.

I was frustrated but I felt frustration was still a positive sign. There was a solution but what we were currently doing was not working out. It was for me to become more flexible, and to start to finding different ways to do what I was doing. Sometimes you want to solve the things soon else they give you more pain even where you smile, and I decidedto try and resolve them. I called her again, she picked my call, cheekiness in her voice, 'You called him again?'

I became despondent. I replied looking at the walls, 'Yes, and you are talking to him, again and again.'

'So?'

Impatiently I was walking in the lawn. In last few minutes mom had asked me to whom I was talking. I hid myself and went to the old room where anyone hardly came. It wasn't store room but it was used to keep old things. I entered hiding my phone. I tried to tell her very softly, looked at the mirror which was half broken and I could see my half face and expected her to be in the reflection.

Reality always has different answers and I moved to the other side, 'Pakhi you are doing wrong and then you are talking like this, is it the right way?' I felt irritated when I again looked at the mirror and kicked it. It fell on the floor and broke into pieces.

'Yeah it's right, I'll do whatever I want, you are no one to stop me. Do whatever you want to do and by breaking things you won't get me.' It seemed she had decided not to talk to me.

Mom shouted from other room, 'What are you doing in that room?'

'Nothing mom, was searching a notebook that I kept last time when I came in holidays, I need that.' While I was answering mom, she disconnected the phone line. She switched off her phone and now I had to catch the culprit. I called Arpan.

'Hello, is Arpan there?'

'Yes, it's Arpan, who's this?'

I replied, anger in my voice, 'It's me, Anuj.'

He replied softly, and it seemed, he tried to be over educated and polite, 'Yes Anuj, say.'

I asked directly, 'What's happening between you and Pakhi?'

He replied, 'Anuj you told me that you are committed but she isn't ready to accept it.'

I said, 'Yes, might be she isn't comfortable with you. She doesn't want to tell, but I am telling you.'

'Then why are you lying that you are committed with her,' he said.

A third person was telling me that and questioning our relationship, That was enough to hurt deeply. How things change, how people change, I could feel that.

'I don't know what she's saying but we are committed from last two years. So please stay away from her,' I said clearly before arguing more.

'Can you prove this?'

'Dude, I don't know you but I know her, and that's enough.'

'Prove it, and I'll never talk to her again,' he started asking to prove it. That was insane.

How it feels when someone asks you to prove you love. I just ignored him.

'Did I fall in love with the same girl, for whom I was everything and for whom I did everything?' I thought for a moment.

I wanted to shout at her.

I touched my face into the mirror, looked at my tears, 'My love is at a stage that it needs a proof in front of an unknown face and who's nothing in front of me.' I thought myself to be the unluckiest guy on this earth.

'What do you want to know, how can I prove it,' I asked and assured him that I was right.

He said very freely, 'She isn't ready to accept anything, you prove it and I'll never talk to her.'

I asked, 'Else?'

He replied proudly, 'Else I'll talk to her because she is my good friend. Can you put your call on conference with her and just talk to her. Or you can do one thing, just record your conversation and send it to me.'

'Sorry, I can't record anything, I know you very well. I can put the call on conference, that's it.' When you don't have solutions and if you get two wrong solutions, one of it looks like a good solution and that time it seems right, in reality it is not. I was trapped in it.

I felt good with the solution but I didn't want to be a cheater, 'I can't prove the way you want me to do that, I'm with her form last two years, I can't do anything like this, I can't cheat on her, sorry.'

'You just talk to her, that's it. I just want to know. That won't be any problem,' he asked. He was normal and polite with his words.

'I can talk to you in front of her but I can't do that, you won't understand,' I replied.

'Hey chill, what's the problem. It's not a big thing. Just add her in the call, I won't speak anything and there is nothing wrong in that. If she is with you, I won't even talk to her,' he actually helped like a friend does.

I tried to make a call on conference with him to solve everything but when bad time comes, it just comes without warning. The moment she picked the call, he spoke over the call, 'what's happening Pakhi?' and he left the call. She also disconnected the call.

My cell phone rang from his call and I picked it. I was just ready to abuse what I was feeling just now and he spoke something which just ruined everything, 'Anuj, now you can't do anything. You are done with her, now it's my time. This is Arpan Ravi, friend of your friend Maddy.'

'What?' current ran in my whole body and for a moment I could see nothing, all black out.

'Yes, game over. I know Maddy, he is my friend and I know each and everything about both of you but she won't trust you anymore. Stay away from her now, she is mine.' He laughed.

'You bastard, asshole, you are just a waste, will see both of you for sure.' I disconnected and felt regretted I could her recorded this conversation but in frustration I could do nothing.

All the dots connected together and I was trapped in a conspiracy created by both of them. Maddy and Apran knew each other. Many times, I noticed Maddy listening to me when I was on call with Pakhi but I ignored him. He started coming to my room frequently and used to ask me if I had someone in my life. All qualms and doubts were clear now. He had told Apran about me and Pakhi months ago. I wanted to tell Pakhi the truth but she was not believing my words anymore.

Things had changed overnight; the promises were broken. Session of college started and next morning I had to leave. This was the most painful journey when I had no one, just broken promises.

```
Pyar he kyun kiya, jab rulana he tha;
Thama he kyun mera haath, jab chhodna he tha.
```

Early morning or late in the night, whenever I called her, her number would be busy.

'Is this love?' I asked myself. Guys don't cry so easily so if they that means that they are hurt and lost.

I called her repeatedly, and after that, she started switching off her cell phone. I remembered each and every moment when we walked together, I remembered her first look, her first touch and her first kiss and tears in my eyes. Again, my eyes became wet and red. I would just turn my face when someone entered my hostel room. I locked the balcony and started crying whenever I missed her.

I wasn't ready to believe that Pakhi didn't want to be with me.

'I trust my love, I trust you God,' I looked at the sky; I pushed my shoulder up. I just pleaded alone, I started begging to get back my love, holding my hands together in prayer, and 'I can't live without her.'

'I need her, please…I need her,' I pleaded alone sitting on the floor.

I remembered that line which I had said when we were in theatre. Pakhi had said-

```
May be the day will come when we will fight but
promise me today that you won't leave me, no
matter where you are.
    I know nobody can love me like this Nobody
can make me feel good. Nobody can make me feel
happy. Nobody can make me cry, So just, love me
forever like this only, because I am only your
baccha. And my reply was same, as it was always-
How can I leave you? I love you; you are the
best. I really love you and I can't live without
you.
```

I stood up and went to my room, and fell on the floor, rubbing my hands; hit my head on the wall for next five minutes. What was love? I came to know when I got injured, blood around me on the floor, both the palms on the floor in the blood, forehead on the wall, just crying for her...for love. My lips were dry, unset hair, half-uncovered body; dry face. It was like crying on someone's death.

It's painful when you are defeated by destiny. Now the only solution I could see was to jump from the balcony to resolve all things. I came in balcony and looked outside, it was dark. I called her once again to say I loved her a lot but she was on call and I crossed my right leg out of the balcony, I thought, 'It is better to die than to live with shame forever.'

'Hey Anuj, what are you doing there?' one of my friends entered the room searching for me, from the back as he couldn't see my blooded and injured forehead.

'Nothing, just looking outside, I am on call with mom, can you come after some time,' I pretended to be funny through my voice.

He responded from the room, 'I thought you are jumping, jump, jump.' And he laughed and lay down on the bed. Still he couldn't see as doors of the balcony were closed. I asked him from outside, 'Then what will happen?'

He said, 'Nothing, if someone jumps from here, there are two possibilities; either you'll die or not. If you die; then nothing, everything is over and out, and if you don't then you will be a loser. Try once,' he laughed and went out of the room.

'If I don't die, then?' the second thought came in my mind.

'I am not a loser, just because few things went wrong, should I finish myself.' By thinking itself it gave me the feeling of being a loser. I came in my room and fell on the bed and started crying.

```
Death seemed easy but I chose to live,
just to tell her how much I loved her.
```

500 Days

If loving you was my mistake, then I'd love to
repeat it for rest of my whole life.

In love of two people, only the patience of one is required. I knew that one day I'd be able to manage everything. I just loved her... nothing else. I knew one thing very well, 'If my love is true, she'll come back in my life for sure.' Once again, I tried to tell her how much I loved her.

It was 15th May 2011 and the next day we were to complete 500 days of this journey which changed us, journey which made us and journey which gave us the reason to be with each other and then suddenly I realized that she didn't want to be with me.

'What were my mistakes?' Flared nostrils, eyes squinting, I was thinking. I didn't know from her end but from my side I was still committed to her. I promised her, at every memorable and adorable day, I'd be in front of her to give her surprises and I didn't want to miss the opportunity to meet her on the 500th day of our relationship.

May be it seems funny and weird to celebrate 500th day or to celebrate the anniversary of first kiss or when you met for the first time. Though it's rare to celebrate first kiss and meeting ceremony at the same day but I actually did that by kissing her on our first meeting.

May be we just stop doing these things by giving a name of mature relationship or long lasting commitment but these things actually need patience, courage and dedication to do something for someone and then keep doing the same forever. We all can fall in love, we all can sleep together, we all can have sex and we can enjoy life but when it comes to be with each other forever, then it actually matters how you look at things.

Without giving any other thought, I decided to go to Delhi to meet her though she wasn't ready to meet me as she was occupied with other things. I never wanted to mention those things.

I was standing outside in front of a book store at CP. She was in college so I preferred to message her because I was trying the best possible way not to disturb her-

```
Hey I am standing in front of Jain Book Depot
in CP.
Can you come here whenever you get time?
Today is the 500th day.
```

Saying 500th day was enough to make her realize how long we have lived together with lots of memories. Though we were not talking to each other but I got her message- Could you come down to Kashmiri Gate?

I reached Kashmiri Gate metro station and waited for some time. After waiting for half an hour, she appeared and that was one of the best moments I had ever lived. I was happy to see her.

We went downstairs and seated at McD which was just next to the metro station. She wasn't looking happy and she had obvious reasons. Wrinkles I could see clearly on her face, she looked tired and dark circles under eyes. I thought she was occupied with her exams, so she didn't take proper sleep. I knew she missed me during her exams as I used to wake her up early morning.

Many of us think that relationship is a responsibility. It's not a responsibility; it's a common way to live together by sharing love, affection, dedication and pain.

Nevertheless, things were changed from her end and she had changed a lot too, that I could hear from her words when she said, sitting on chair, 'Anuj! Please try to understand that I can't be with you.'

I looked into her eyes and then looked around. I didn't want to hear that, 'what happened Pakhi, why are you saying all this? If you need some time then we can think about it but please don't say like this.'

'I don't think so it's possible for me to be with you anymore, we have fought enough. I think we have crossed our limits and started disrespecting each other. I don't want to do that, so please leave me alone and don't call me too much.'

I opened the zip of my bag and gave her favourite chocolate and beautiful card which I made last night for her with a long message on the back side of it and on the front side butterflies with romantic messages on their wings. I didn't want to read, I wanted her to read herself and feel how much I loved her. She smiled but her face wasn't glowing as I saw when I met her last time. 'Hey, we have completed 500 days today and this is for you,' I tried to look into her eyes and whispered, 'I love you.'

'No, but I don't want. Please try to understand and leave me alone. And I can't take this card because if someone would see it, it would be a problem for me,' she read few lines of it and she forced herself to stand up.

'Okay but please keep this chocolate at least.'

She smiled and took it. Again I tried to say, touching her hand, 'I love you and I don't want to leave you.'

'Anuj but it's not possible,' she looked at me, moved ahead and left...

No Replay, No Rewind

Why god has given me these rude friends? I said on my first birthday in college, when my friends were giving me birthday bumps. Now I was searching for at least one person to share my pain and feelings with and I was helpless. Time changed, people changed and my life had changed.

That video was still in the folder named win32 that I made for her. Now that was enough to make me cry. I was still alive. I could breathe. I could eat. I could walk, nevertheless, when I breathed there was no fragrance in the air, when I ate I chewed a bite for long, when I walked, my legs pulled me back. Days were so long and every night made me cry. Now my phone never rang with romantic ringtone. There were no romantic messages in inbox of my cell phone. I stopped replying to any messages from my friends, forgot to carry my phone because who would I carry it for? I had compromised everything when she was with me now I had nothing with me.

I loved to sleep but now I started hating nights and my bed. Suddenly I used to wake up in the night missing her, and would start crying because whenever I dialled her number either she was busy or she didn't pick the call. Smile, it seemed I just forgot how to do that. Every day I cried, looking here and there in the room in scrape, walked and again came to my bed, I would start crying but nobody was there to listen to me and then I ended up keeping pillow on my head and spending nights like that. The voice-mails she sent me and which

I saved in my laptop, I just used to listen to them in loop for nights and just cried looking at the photographs. Sometimes I tried to hate them to feel better but I couldn't. I just shouted alone in the room. Hit myself to the walls and slept just with my tears and wet pillow. I used to walk at 3 o'clock in the night as I felt I am alone in the world and…LONELY. I logged on my laptop to see her photographs early in the morning and checked mails expecting that someday she'll mail me a voice mail to give me surprise but I forgot; nobody was missing me, nobody was there to even look at me.

I had deleted all romantic movies from my laptop. I had deleted all songs, everything but not that video which I made for her. I used to watch that video all the time. I would go to the long voicemail to play again and again. I closed my eyes and tried to feel that she was in front of me and kissing me on my cheeks; holding my hands and whispering I love you, I'll never leave you. Nevertheless, when I came across the reality, I again closed my eyes but this time to hide my tears. I just hugged my pillow whenever I missed her. My life had become porous. Nothing was left in my life, everything seemed over and finished. I tried to sleep on time but I couldn't as there were no night talks and calls. I checked my phone so many times and waited for her messages and calls but every time I washed my tears. I sat somewhere in the corner of the room and thought about everything that happened between us. Sometimes not even a single tear ran down my cheeks, my tears had dried; I was too hurt.

Wadon ka mahal , iradon ki ek tasveer bnayi thi,
Tere hathon me rakh, apne hathon ki lakeer bnayi thi;
Yun umeed na thi achanak, mehal khandhar me badal jayega,
Jo bhi bnayi thi humne , apni jindgi ko teri jageer banayi thi;

```
Wo safar wo karvan wo manjil tak humsfar bane
rhne ka wada bhi kiya tha tumne,
Par afsos ki tumne dhage ki tarah toda;
aur humne use zindgi ke dariya ko par karne ki
zanjeer banayi thi.
```

Everything else had gone with her, my dreams, my happiness, my smile, my feelings, my future and a lot more. I had changed a lot. I was a guy who always had fun with my friends but now my friends had started saying, 'What happened Anuj, are you ok?'

I just showed them my fake smile now. I had learnt to wear a fake smile but it was tough and painful. Whenever I tried to be happy and smile, I remembered all those happy moments with Pakhi, missed her alto and felt like crying. I stopped to pick calls and when my mom called me, I washed my face so she couldn't understand that I had been crying.

When she asked me, 'What happened *beta*, are you crying?'

'No, mom, having cold from last night, that's why. I am perfectly fine, how are you?' and after disconnecting the call I just cried aloud in bed remembering all those moments that I spent with Pakhi.

I started living alone and isolated, when my friends talked to me; I started shouting at them. My friendship went in the wrong way and I lost most of my friends. Nobody wanted to talk to me because nobody knew anything.

The Last Message

This I never expected. The last day when I met her on the 500th day in Delhi, she put a letter in my bag when I went to take a glass of water, I made a guess. I was happy to see the letter but it was painful when I went through it. The letter said-

Hi Anuj,

Please read this patiently. You are a nice person or rather I'd say you are a dream person for any girl; nobody could love anyone as you loved me. Now I hope you deserve a better girl than me in your life. My life has changed a lot in just last few months. I lost my father, and I could have seen him if I wasn't with you that day when I got a call and we were in bed but I couldn't. I lost friends who used to pamper me. Now they hate me because I compared their friendship with your love and you won every time, and slowly and gradually I lost them. I don't know whether things will be fine one day or not but I am not meant to face these situations in life.

Mentally and physically, I have lost my senses. Neither I can feel anything nor smell.

I am not blaming anyone, I just want to go away from everyone and I can't be with you anymore.

I can't see my mom crying all the time sitting in the corner of the room; I need to fix few things. I don't know how will I manage but I'll try to get her days back. If destiny has any plans for us then we will meet again but I don't know how true it is so better forget me and please move on in your life. Many people come in our lives and they go away. You came in my life to make me feel what is love but I think I wasn't that lucky to carry it forever.

You always used to ask about that mail which I sent to Ajay. I don't love anyone else. The mail you saw in my mail box which was sent to ajay 16...@gmail.com was my mistake that I realized because I needed peace but the more I searched for it, the more lost I was and ended up with nothing.

I can't love anyone else except you in my life. I am also a human being, I also have feelings. I just loved you and will love you forever.

All the best, be a successful person and don't change yourself because you're the inspiration of love, life and dedication.

Wherever you're reading this, I am waiting for a tight hug. Love you and take care.

Your love.

I kept holding my breath, was reading and remembering those moments. If you're mad for something, it comes to you for sure. I had faith in my love that someday she'd come back in my life. She was nowhere on G-mail, Facebook or any other social media. I called her on her number that didn't exist anymore. I tried all her numbers but no use. I was helpless. If I tried to mail her, they would bounce. Many of my friends told me to move on because they couldn't see my pain. However, I never wanted to move on. I didn't want to be the part of the crowd where people love and forget. I loved once and I had to live once.

Nothing Left to Lose -
A Month Later

My tears had dried up and I was alone even in the most crowded places. It's difficult to smile when it doesn't come from your heart. Therefore, I reached home next morning. Over the last few days, I had realized it's tough to live for me so I thought it would be difficult for her too and she would come back but nothing like that happened. It was more than a month, I was trying her cell phone but it wasn't reachable. I left a message for her-

Are you happy without me? Would you celebrate
your birthday without me? Without you, everything
is incomplete. I have only your e-mails, which
you sent to me after our fights to make me feel
happy again. I know that it is you who shouted
many times but now even I am missing all that,
please come back.

Tears were rolling on my cheeks and then dropped on my finger before I clicked one of her old e-mails that she sent me months ago-

Hi Anuj,

Please read this mail with patience, Anuj I know
we had lots of fights in last few days. I wanted
to share lots of things with you. Anuj, I know

I'm the reason of all the fights but this is
true that I love you a lot more than anyone in
my life. Whenever I changed myself for our love
then something went wrong and then I stopped
doing anything for our relation. Anuj, I love
you a lot and I want you to be happy. Please
remove from your mind that I want to leave you.
Why would I leave you?

We love each other so much and there is
no reason to leave. A guy who takes care of
everything in my life, why would I leave him. A
girl wants a caring, understanding, loving guy
in her life and you complete me. It's a dream
for a girl to be with you.

Anuj, you are the one who wakes me up early
in the morning, who sings for me before I go to
sleep, who makes me laugh whenever I feel sad
and who makes me cry with his lovely surprises.
You pamper me like a small child as my dad used
to do; that's why sometimes I talked to you
very rudely but I really love you. Truly I'm
nothing without you Anuj. I can't even imagine
my life without you. I want your support. Hope
after reading this, we will have a tight hug.
I'm waiting for your hug.

Your Loving, Pakhi

I went through each and every lines multiple times. I took the
card which I made for her when I met her on the 500th day of our
relationship. She didn't accept that time saying that someone would

catch her with this card at home. I started going through it once again with wet eyes and dry hopes to get her back in my life.

Hi Pakhi, I know you don't love me anymore. If you loved me, then you would have wiped the tears in my eyes. When you came to EDM mall to meet me, you looked tired.

You're like a small girl. You should take care of yourself. I saw those dark circles around your eyes. Your lips were dry. You were acting to be happy, but I know, you were not.

You did nothing like that; instead you left like always without any apologies or goodbyes. You hurt me so badly with all your lies. I did nothing but cried, thinking that everything was a joke to you. You took advantage of my love, my feelings, and my emotions.

Today I just want to ask you if it was all worth it. I promised you a life of love and happiness and instead gave you nothing but pain and sorrow. We both hurt each other. The only difference is that when you were with someone else, you were lost, confused, and hurt. You had no idea what you were doing and why you were doing it. Should I really forgive you?

Well, I already have. You know why, because I love you. When you love someone so much, like I love you, you don't look at the bad stuff someone did to you. I'm blinded by all the good times, all the times that you put a smile on my face and just how happy your presence in my life made me. I know you haven't forgiven me otherwise you would smile and look into my eyes (I was seeing you and you looked into my eyes full of tears, and now you say you hate me. You love me my baby.) I love you today the same way I loved you two years before. I love you today as I'll love you every day from now. My love isn't fake. My love is mature enough and understands everything now. One day you'll realize that I love you and have always loved you.

I didn't say anything because I wanted to see your eagerness. After a long fight, I know you missed me a lot.

Your eagerness to meet me, your eagerness to talk to me was on your face but you were lying that you are getting late and you have to leave.

I know you are very kind hearted; I'm waiting to see that.

I love you!!! Miss you a lot. Please come back in my life.

Hey, don't cry baby. You are my baccha, you know this na. Your backbone is waiting for your call. First get up, have some water, and wash your face. You know you are so stupid. No need to cry ok, I love you a lot.

Your backbone, Anuj

I had started writing in that diary and suddenly I came into reality when Rashmi informed that I was suffering from hypertension as per her observations and reports. Doctor Rashmi was my family doctor. That was the reason my family took me to the hospital. Rashmi was one of those very few people who knew about my life and problems. They were saying that I was not treated well culturally that's why it happened to me. *Falling in love is like a sin in this society.* People start making obligations the moment you fail in your life. There are very few people who become your support and help you to stand again.

Doctors had already said that I had to increase my doses of medicine without negative vibes around. I also had told them that instead of putting efforts in making me better they should talk to her and call her here. From last 19 days doctor Rashmi was the ward-in-charge and being family doctor she had gone through my reports and my life. I was just afraid if she would tell my family everything about me. 'Anuj, you just need to take care of yourself, everything will be fine,' she put her hand on my head. 'Is this is critical stage of hypertension?' I asked her. I wanted to smile the way she took care of me but I felt so tired to stretch my lips.

'Who said this?' she said as if she didn't hear what I said or as if she didn't have an answer.

'Those nurses who come early morning for cleaning,' I said and closed my eyes.

'I am MBBS from KGMC, gold medallist throughout the year, hope this is enough to put your trust on me,' she smiled, writing something on report file.

'Why am I feeling like I just want to sleep and there will be no pain if I sleep forever.'

She just ignored me and again I asked her, 'Hey doctor, do people die if they love someone truly,' my dry face and wet eyes made her eyes wet too.

'You are this best guy I have ever seen. You have lost six kilograms in a fortnight. I just want you to think positive and take care.' She held my hand and she looked as if she wanted to say something but she stopped.

'Did you love someone in your life?' I asked her.

'I was in a relationship for four years and when I started insisting him for marriage, he started fighting. I understood what was going on for four years...,' she stopped in between and said; 'now let's stop this and take rest. It's 3 pm, your mom must be coming.'

'Doctor, I promise, I'll be fine. Just one request I have if I can use my laptop.'

'I can't allow you Anuj, you need to take rest, so sleep properly and get well soon.'

'Please, just for few hours in a day and tell my family too that I can use else dad shouts. I actually want to write everything and...'

'And what...' she asked surprisingly.

'I will tell you one day.'

She left the ward.

She used to say that our journey was different from other love stories, so the title I wrote on the top 'Journey of Two Hearts' and I started writing and shuffling the notes, messages and chats to include the story of our life. Now I had a hopeful reason to wake up early morning to write those moments we spent together and few other things that happened to me and about those people who tried to break us. For a fortnight it went on like I wanted it to be. I Slept sitting on the head side of the bed, holding the diary in my hand and laptop on the other side. I woke up suddenly due to some unpleasant noise in dreams. The clock said 1:30 p.m.

Rashmi allowed me to go home. 'Mr. Tiwari, from tomorrow you can enjoy at home,' doctor Rashmi announced in the ward. I half opened my eyes and tried to look at her. I rounded my tongue around the lips my mouth felt dry. I was in depression for the last one month but now I was better though I was still suffering.

'You are perfect now,' she said, coming to my head side. She looked at me and tried to make me happy.

'Your RBC (Red Blood Cells), WBC (White Blood Cells), Electrolytes, Liver function, and Kidney function, everything is just perfect,' she looked at me, placed her hand on my forehead.

'Weight is 56 kilogram which is not good Anuj,' she grinned and added, 'So better have whatever you want no prescription for that.'

I smiled partially.

'But doctor, would I be able to get my old days back?' tears in her eyes but she didn't allow them to come out in front of me. Mom entered.

'How are you my *beta?*' mom asked.

'Hm...now I won't trouble this rude doctor and tomorrow I can come home,' I smiled; doctor and mom both looked at me. They looked happy.

'Yes, Anuj can go with you tomorrow, he is perfect now and that's my duty not to allow you to stay awake till late night, so I have to be rude,' she smiled and talked something to mom.

Mom sat on the left side of the bed and placed her hand on my feet. 'What are you doing mom?' I asked. There were moments when I used to make her sleep peacefully and used to massage her head and legs. So it was awkward for me when she touched my legs. I could feel her emotions. I tried to sit taking support of the wall and I was fighting myself to sit, there were tears in mom's eyes. She didn't say anything and wiped her tears.

'Mom, what happened, why are you crying?' I said, and made myself strong not to cry in front of her.

'I love you beta, you are everything for me, without you I can't live,' mom said and I had broken into tears because it was difficult for me to hide my pain anymore. I wanted to tell her each and everything I felt and wanted to spend some time in her arms.

'I love you too mom, you are the best mother in the world,' tears were wetting my cheeks and she was wiping my cheeks from her hands. I was fighting with my own thoughts which were hurting me that I did everything to get back my love, even lied to my mother, and neither she is with me nor I can look into my mother's eyes.

Wiping her tears, mom said, 'Get up and have something. You are the best son.' Mom came to my side. I pointed her to my head to sit there, 'Yes, tell *beta*.' I felt like I didn't have courage to say anything.

'Mom, I want to hug you,' I broke aloud into tears and mom hugged me tightly. The moment she hugged, I remembered all those moments when she used to pamper me and motivate me when I would be upset. I cried as much as I could and by doing that I could feel love after so many years. I didn't know what and where I was but whatever it was, I lived my life in her arms.

'I am always with you. Don't cry,' she patted and ran her hands in my hair, and wiped my tears and her tears too.

'I am sorry, mom. I know I have done so many mistakes. Please forgive me. I promise you that I wouldn't do anything. I made you cry. I lied. I hurt you.' I held both the hands tightly and kept on my chest, and closed my eyes, pressed as hard as I could.

'How can't I forgive you?' my eyes were full of tears.

'Mom, you gave me everything in my life but you never asked me to pay back. You are the best mom in this world,' I said wetting her hands with my tears. Mothers are like that.

I could see tears in Rashmi's eyes. 'Doctor, why are you crying?' I smiled.

'Stupid you are,' doctor Rashmi said.

I wasn't sure but I made a guess that Doctor Rashmi told something about it to my mom. However, my mom didn't ask me anything about her.

Next day early in the morning, Doctor Rashmi came into my ward.

'Anuj, this is your last morning here,' she smiled.

'I can live here forever, should I?' I asked doctor Rashmi.

'No need, I don't love you now, you have to leave,' she replied looking at the reports, turning pages.

At the next moment, 'You want to say something,' Rashmi asked looking at me. I nodded.

She came to me, 'Everything will be fine, okay, don't worry. I was also just like you few years back. I'm doctor now and treat people like you, hope someday you'll teach others. So be brave and do something so that people can feel proud of you. But no need to come here again,' she smiled again, blinked her eyes.

'You are 30. I'm 21, nine years difference we have. Does it matter to you or should I talk to my mom about you?' we both tried to laugh.

'Anuj, she is your doctor,' mom said.

'Mom I like this doctor, nine years difference matters to you?' I tilted my neck and took a water bottle as my throat was dried up now.

'That's perfectly fine but for now we need to leave,' mom said.

Doctor and mom talked for some time. I didn't know what they were talking about. However, they were surely talking about me.

A cab came to the hospital and we all left for home.

Epilogue:
Three Months Later

I was trying to start my life in the city of dreams, Mumbai, as a software professional. We both planned to come to Mumbai but I came and she didn't.

I was on the way back from office, my cell phone flashed with Anushka's call. I picked her call. Without saying anything, she just asked, 'So did you get any publisher for the book?'

'Seven publishers have already rejected, few more are yet to reply. I don't think any of them wants to publish it else they could have given a thought at least discuss with me,' I had lost hopes the way I was getting rejections from publishers.

'Yeah, I have searched about it on Google, and I think it should be purely commercial. So, they didn't even discuss about it?' she asked.

'No, they didn't. I don't want to get it published, that's not my wish, I just want her back in my life or at least I can tell her through this book that I need her back in my life. I talked to one printing press in Noida. They are ready to print a thousand copies but they need eighty percent payment in advance and after calculating all my savings, it will take few more months to save,' I still had hopes that my book will reach in her hands one day.

'What is the actual problem, why are they rejecting it? Don't they know your genuine reason to get it published,' she asked something that even I didn't know.

'I think, they are not interested in true stories and it's not commercially fit for them, but it's okay. Printer said that he'll print for me with good quality,' tears were in my eyes because this world never cares about your emotions, they do what they have to and it's perfectly fine. Everyone has to face the reality of life.

'One day surely you'll get what you wish for, just take care of yourself and hope you're taking your medicines,' she said and continued, 'So when are you coming to Delhi?'

'Next month Navya has her engagement ceremony, so probably I'll come to Delhi.' Something struck in my mind and I said, 'Anushka if we distribute printouts of this book in colleges in Delhi, this might be able to reach in her hands someday.'

I had suggested her before but we couldn't execute because it seemed impractical but I didn't want to leave any stone unturned. I never wanted to regret that I didn't try. So for next two months, every Saturday I used to go to Delhi University and distribute few chapters of this book to people just outside the gate of Delhi University. After so many rejections, it got a reason to get it published as a book. Perhaps to finally reach her hands some day.

```
The sweetness of LOVE only you can taste after
wetting your lips with tears. In life, at least
once a person comes in your life and changes you
for the rest of your life, just like a potter
who takes clay, gives it a proper shape and puts
it into fire. After that, it is not possible
to come back in the natural form...LOVE IS JUST
LIKE THAT and I was not untouched with that
reality of life.
```

Author's Note

Before you close the book, I just want to say thanks for you living my life through this book. I apologize if I have made you cry. It was painful for me to jot down those moments which I never wanted to share with anyone, but sometimes we need to take a few steps in life to get life back.

We shouldn't leave hope for love, life, family and friendship, if our feelings are true. Things always happen for a reason and I believe true love still exists because we both loved truly. Hope someday this book will reach in her hands and she will come back to me.

Let me take an oath – if this book reaches in her hands, I'd surely write something after this. Else you can forget me, considering that there was a guy who loved truly, but was defeated by his destiny. Thanks for being a part of my *Journey of Two Hearts!*

You can write to me at anujtiwari.official@gmail.com.

Printed in Great Britain
by Amazon.co.uk, Ltd.,
Marston Gate.